Light Chaser

ALSO BY GARETH L. POWELL

ALSO BY PETER F. HAMILTON

THE CHRONICLE OF THE FALLERS
The Abyss Beyond Dreams
Night Without Stars

THE QUEEN OF DREAMS
The Secret Throne
The Hunting of the Princes
A Voyage Through Air

THE SALVATION SEQUENCE
Salvation
Salvation Lost
The Saints of Salvation

THE ARKSHIP TRILOGY (AUDIO)
A Hole in the Sky

STANDALONE NOVELS
Fallen Dragon
Watching Trees Grow
Great North Road

COLLECTIONS
A Second Chance at Eden
Manhattan in Reverse
The Confederation Handbook

LIGHT CHASER

PETER F. HAMILTON
AND GARETH L. POWELL

A TOM DOHERTY ASSOCIATES BOOK

NEW YORK

LIGHT CHASER

Cover art by Ben Zweifel
Cover design by Christine Foltzer

Edited by Lee Harris

A Tordotcom Book
Published by Tom Doherty Associates
120 Broadway
New York, NY 10271

www.tor.com

Tor® is a registered trademark of
Macmillan Publishing Group, LLC.

ISBN 978-1-250-76981-7 (ebook)
ISBN 978-1-250-76982-4 (trade paperback)

First Edition: August 2021

To our families, decent people who through no fault of their own have to live in the same house as writers

Take this kiss upon the brow!
And, in parting from you now,
Thus much let me avow—
You are not wrong, who deem
That my days have been a dream

Edgar Allen Poe,
"A Dream Within A Dream" (1849)

I

AMAHLE COULD NO LONGER remember how old she was. Born human and later imbued with synthetic eight-letter DNA, she was always destined to have a lifespan measured in millennia. Then she found herself flying the *Mnemosyne* around and around a loop of The Domain's settled worlds at close to the speed of light, so time compression made her effectively immortal to any observer. But the night before she died, she said: "I think I'm finally scared."

"Don't worry," Carloman said. "It will be so quick, not even *your* nerves can send a pain signal into your brain."

She clung to him in the webbing envelope as the mini-bots slowly broke up the last extraneous parts of the cabin around them, shrinking it further. "That wasn't quite what I meant. It's not the pain, it's death itself."

"There is nothing to fear. Trust me, I remember all my deaths."

"I'll try," she said, and gripped him tighter, pressing her face into his skin as if extra comfort might be found there. "Really I will."

She had adored her shipboard life ever since it began, whenever it began back in those time-lost circumstances. *Mnemosyne* was the sleek end product of a society at the height of its technological prowess, a starship that travelled at point-nine-seven lightspeed between the inhabited worlds of The Domain. Its two-kilometre length resembled a thick silver spear as it slipped through interstellar space, a design flourish only the indolence of a true post-scarcity world would bother with. In space, alone and unseen in a bubble of relativity distorted time, there was really no need for aesthetics. Yet its designers had given it a cloak of fluxfabrik like viscid quicksilver that flowed protectively over the long gantry spine of struts which held its component modules together: life support, big enough to carry a hundred passengers in considerable luxury; engineering with its half-million integrated systems maintained by semi-sentient bots and a cluster of manufactories; a hangar where its subsidiary craft rested between star systems; tanks, plenty of those, containing both fuel and matter reserves for the manufactories; and generator stacks providing the phenomenal quantity of energy required by the final module, the negative-matter drive. All of this perfect machinery was controlled by a full-sentient-rated AI, guiding it unerringly across interstellar space on voyages that lasted for years of ship-time and decades of real-time.

Amahle, who'd been its captain and sole occupant for thousands of years as she flew around and around the loop, had relished the wonders and miseries which human civilizations were capable of. It was a perfect life for someone of her origin. Experiencing the lives of others from the safety and solitude of the gulf between stars.

Was.

Had been.

Used to be.

———

Now the *Mnemosyne* was a very different beast as it approached the subgiant star three thousand light years from the outermost worlds of The Domain. No longer slim and streamlined, the silver fluxfabrik cloak had morphed out into a broad umbrella with the transformed starship nestled in its shade, where it was protected from near-lightspeed particle impact. For the last two years of the fifteen-year voyage, a swarm of engineering bots had been industriously restructuring the ancient starship. The hangar with all its surface-to-orbit shuttles and trans-planetary craft had gone, converted into raw mass along with every other superfluous component, to be stored as plasma in big magnetic confinement chambers. That included the palatial life support module, which had slowly been fed into the matter refineries over the final six months of approach. No longer did Amahle have vast compartments of every environment from tropical to polar; the swimming aquarium was long gone, as were the med-clinic and faux eighteenth-century-Earth aristocrat's dining hall. Life support had shrunk down to a ten-metre sphere, with very basic utilities. Over the last month, the matter refineries had even devoured their own engineering section in a final act of cybernetic cannibalism. All these alterations had reduced the *Mnemosyne* to an errant clutter of globes ribbed with big flow ducts, transparent pipes that replaced the original gantry in a woven helix of glowing plasma, as if the starship were somehow surrounded by machine DNA.

———————

Amahle woke on the last morning and smiled at Carloman, who was still in the webbing envelope next to her. He smiled back at her.

"Are you sure about this?" he asked.

"I think that's what I should be asking you, isn't it? And anyway, whoever asks, they should have done it fifteen years ago, before we started."

"Touché."

They both wriggled out of the webbing. Amahle found the stk bag with her dress in. Peeled it off the wall and opened it. There were no other clothes left, wardrobes the size of houses had all been transformed into plasma.

"Nice," Carloman observed as she put it on. "You look gorgeous, but then you always do, every time." There was moisture in his eyes as he spoke.

She'd picked the garment up centuries before from a world on the loop that was forever poised on the cusp between totalitarian barbarism and the steam age. It was beautiful, lush red silk that moved like oil, hand-tailored to her unchanging figure, elegant and sophisticated, as well as subtly enticing. "The perfect definition of overdressing for the occasion," she told him. "But I wanted to go out in style."

"Mission accomplished."

"When you say things like that, so full of meaning, I never know if you're quoting some famous deep-history person or not."

"Quoting, but very out of context."

They kissed.

"Let's get on with it," she said levelly. Even so, she was shaking slightly as they strapped themselves into the acceleration couches on the wall opposite the bathroom chamber.

"Three-sixty visual," she told the *Mnemosyne's* network. It wasn't a sentient AI anymore, not since she'd killed the high-level routines decades before. But it operated the diminished starship's functions effectively, obediently following her commands.

The little cabin's walls vanished, replaced by the external sensor feeds. Two acceleration couches sped through space at point-nine-four lightspeed. Behind them was a small patch of red mist, all the stars they were racing away from, including the vast area of space containing The Domain. Ahead was a single point of painfully intense blue light: the subgiant. Between the two, bracketing the couches, was a darkness even Amahle, with all her centuries of space travel experience, found unnerving.

"We're about twenty hours out," she said as navigational graphics slid over her vision. "It's going to get bumpy now."

He grinned. "Finally, something that's physical."

The *Mnemosyne* was coming in twenty degrees south of the subgiant's ecliptic, a vector which kept them clear of all the planets, asteroids, comets, and dust that orbited around the star's equatorial band. But even so, the density of particles grew as they closed on the huge star. Their curving silver shield had been glowing a faint violet for over a year as it repelled interstellar gas and the occasional larger clump of carbon molecules that struck them. Now the glow started to increase as they streaked inwards, exerting a weak braking force against the starship's terrific velocity. The negative-matter drive increased thrust to compensate.

Amahle pulled two of the subgiant's planets up out of the visual and studied the associated datafield. "Some interesting chemical activity in those atmospheres," she observed as the cloud-wrapped globes hung before them. "Very non-terrestrial. Which one is it, do you think?"

"I have no idea what form The Exalted might take. See, you're being too conventional looking in the terrestrial life band. They could be evolving on one of the cryoplanets, or maybe floating through the star's corona."

"Not for much longer," she said. As she'd done countless times every day of the mission, she checked the stasis vault. The datafield reassured her the strangelet particle they were carrying at the heart of the *Mnemosyne* remained stable.

At a hundred AUs out, the glow of atoms rupturing around the silver shield was expanding, stretching out behind them like a flickering cometary tail. Amahle had already felt the starship shudder several times as they smashed into solar debris massing several grams. The resultant detonations were like fusion bombs going off against the fluxfabrik. Their velocity punched them through, putting the blast tens of thousands of kilometres behind them in milliseconds. But the shield suffered, ablation carnage ripping away huge segments of its quasi-solid structure. The thick flow ducts twined around the ship responded instantly, shunting plasma up to reinforce the depleted fluxfabrik shield at near-lightspeed, their radiance rivalling the impact plumes for brightness.

"I'm surprised we're still here," Amahle said. "Surely, The Exalted will just change this reality?"

"Reality is what we perceive it to be."

"You mean we're willing this to happen?"

"Not exactly, the physical universe we perceive has an inertia all of its own, the rules, if you like. Time seems to be a constant within it; even we are governed by that while we're here. Think of this flight as playing chess with causality. And this, the end, is our checkmate move."

"No matter what, I'm glad I found you again," she told him sincerely.

"We always find each other."

"You're a romantic."

"Yes."

"No, really, a romantic. You believe love is a universal constant, too." She looked across at him. Seeing him in profile against the tortured breath of the shield's impact flare, his eyes closed, lips lifted serenely.

"Of course, how else do you explain us?" he said.

———

At forty AUs out, the buffeting had increased dramatically.

It took considerable effort for Amahle not to grip the edge of the acceleration couch in an attempt to hold still. Maybe wearing the dress had been a bad idea.

"We're past the outer cryoplanet," Carloman said. "Five hours to go."

"I wonder if they'll go fast or slow."

"Perception is your—"

"Yes! I get it."

"Think of it as a whole lifetime."

"Ha! Even mayflies have longer than this."

"When did you last see a mayfly?"

"I'm not sure I ever have." She gave him a brittle grin. "Maybe I remembered it from before. Some things are sharper than they have been for years."

"That's good. That means death is approaching."

"You really know how to cheer a girl up."

———

The *Mnemosyne*'s damage tail grew brighter and longer as they drew closer to the subgiant, the rip of atomic ruin taking longer to decay, it was so violent. A rigid strand of actinic light stretched out for almost half an AU behind the starship now, its tip a glare point to rival the star it was approaching. In the life support cabin, the noise of the solar wind impacting against the fluxfabrik shield had become so loud, talking was almost impossible. The severe shaking made the display judder to a chaotic blur, reducing the datafield to chaos. But there was no mistaking the steadily brightening subgiant directly ahead, expanding out from a speck to a small intense disk.

"Five minutes," Amahle shouted. She wriggled an arm free of the restraint straps, reaching out—

Something large, probably a rock chunk massing a kilogram, struck the fluxfabrik shield. The vicious detonation shock wave transmitted through what was left of the starship pummelled the life support cabin. Amahle screamed as her arm was wrenched round painfully. Carloman caught her hand, and they gripped each other tightly. Outside, the plasma ducts surged, brightening to primordial levels as they fed reinforcements to the shield.

Amahle grimaced at the forward image. The subgiant was inflating rapidly now, a circular expanse of light that was a quarter of her vision. A half. Rushing towards them—

"This is a seriously bad idea," she yelled. Tried to laugh, but all she could do was cry.

Carloman squeezed her hand tighter. "I'm here. I'm never going to let go of you—"

They were facing each other when the *Mnemosyne* reached the outer fringes of the corona. The density of the solar ejecta overwhelmed the fluxfabrik shield in milliseconds. *Mnemosyne* didn't explode, there simply wasn't time, it instantaneously transformed to vapour. A plume that was still travelling relativistically as it swept past the roiling prominences as they rode rogue magnetic flux lines. It pierced the chromosphere like a phantom arrow, stabbing further down into the photosphere. That was where it finally lost cohesion as it briefly created a splash crater a thousand kilometres wide through the elemental soup.

The stasis vault disintegrated along with the rest of the starship, liberating the strangelet. But not even the vast outpouring of plasma and light of a star could repel the cataract of atomic wreckage travelling a mere fraction under lightspeed. The unnatural cluster of quarks punctured the convection zone.

As it shot deeper and deeper into the subgiant, the strangelet finally struck an atomic nucleus, catalysing its transformation into strange matter. The energy release generated a larger, more stable strangelet. It hit another nucleus, another conversion, another infinitesimal growth in size occurred.

The subgiant had a diameter of just over three million kilometres. To convert the entire mass of a star that large took time. But the strangelet's alchemy was exponential. For the first century, there was no noticeable effect. Then the surface began to distort, sunspots bloomed and multiplied as the magnetic flux lines were warped out of alignment.

The internal anomaly began to devour the rest of the ordinary matter at a rate which quickly outstripped the fusion process. Towards the end, energy creation rose at a phenomenal rate, creating an exceptionally fierce emission of ultra-hard radiation. Future alien astronomers across the galaxy would see the final explosion as a supernova of unusual potency and wonder at its cause.

The effect of the detonation on the subgiant's planets was as devastating as Carloman had hoped. Its initial pulse of radiation hit the two gas giants, flash-evaporating their upper atmospheres to send continent-sized plumes writhing out into space. The lower atmosphere immediately started to decompress to replace the loss, which in turn liberated the ultra-volatile liquid layers beneath in a progression that ended in both cores rupturing, adding their force to the cataclysm. Cryoplanets burned, the small solid worlds shattered.

As the haze of the supernova's detonation wavefront darkened and dissipated across interstellar space, the full scale of the destruction was revealed. There was no planetary system anymore, only a zone of total annihilation with a small, radio-silent husk at the centre. The quark star: with its outer shell of neutronium containing differentiated layers of quark material, which in turn formed a prison around the core of strange matter. A prison which would shield its secret composition until the heat death of the universe.

II

THE SIGHT OF THE cat stopped Amahle in her tracks. It lay curled on the wooden countertop of one of the hastily erected market stalls, between the buckets of apples and blackberries the merchant had brought in this morning on his cart. Sleek and black with white paws, the animal seemed oblivious to the commercial tumult around it—the livestock; the laughter of children splashing through the mud; the chatter of men and women browsing and haggling over the various wares on display; and the ever-present sound of rain dripping from the canvas awning.

She could barely remember the last time she'd seen a cat with her own eyes. It must have been a couple of circuits before—so, at least two thousand years—and several dozen light years closer to the Central Worlds. She hadn't even known there were any here on Winterspite. But then, given their medieval technology, she supposed they needed something reliable to guard the fruit and grain stores from rats and other vermin. Rats had travelled between the stars to every world in The Domain;

even the post-scarcity worlds had them.

"What's its name?" she asked in the local tongue, reaching out to tickle the animal behind its ear. The stall-holder blinked at her with rheumy eyes.

"I just call him 'cat.'"

"Is he yours?"

"I reckon so. Much as a cat belongs to anyone."

"Is he for sale?"

The man scratched his beard. "I don't know. Nobody's ever asked to buy him before."

Amahle reached inside her cloak and brought out a couple of coins. "I'll give you two gold florins for him."

To his credit, the stallholder kept a straight face; the man would have made an intimidatingly good poker player. Two florins represented more wealth than he would likely see in an entire season. "Lady," he said, "you've got a deal." He fetched a wicker basket from his cart, placed the cat inside, and fastened the lid.

"I keep him in here when we're traveling," he explained.

"Thank you." Amahle passed over the coins and took the basket in return. The little transaction had begun to draw a crowd. People were watching curiously, whispering to each other. Beneath her woollen cloak Amahle wore an ancient orange dress, which was made from cotton, a fabric plentiful enough on Winterspite, so she should've blended in without trouble. But the vivid colour acted like a beacon among the muted tones worn by the general populace. That along with the fact she had all her teeth made it very clear she wasn't from around these parts.

"Hang on." The stallholder frowned, as if seeing her properly for the first time. He looked her up and down. "You're *her,* aren't you?"

Amahle sighed. She'd wanted the chance for a bit of a look around before announcing herself at the palace. After all, these people had been waiting a thousand years for her to come back; she'd thought another couple of hours wouldn't hurt. But now, once everyone knew she was there, they'd start acting on their best behaviour, trying to impress her or to curry favour, and she'd lose the opportunity to experience the culture firsthand, through her own eyes. Though *culture* might be stretching it . . .

"I might be."

"You are, though."

"Yeah."

The merchant looked down at the money in his palm, then clenched his fingers over it as if it might turn to dust and blow away.

"Holy hell," he said. "You're the Light Chaser."

"And you just sold me a cat for two gold florins."

Amahle glanced around at the onlookers. "They'll probably write songs about you."

———————

With her cover blown, Amahle had little choice but to make her way to the Golden Keep at the centre of town, where she formally announced herself to the guards, and was shown in to the throne room.

The last time she'd been there, a thousand years previously, the ruler had been a hairy brute who went by the soubriquet Olaf the Butcher. This time around, a young woman occupied the throne. Her name was Gloriana. She had long white hair and delicate features, but her eyes were so flint-like you could probably have struck sparks from them.

"Your Highness," Amahle said formally, bowing her head but not her knee, "I have returned to trade to our mutual benefit. I'm gladdened to see how much the kingdom has prospered under your rule; so much has improved since my last visit."

The queen gripped the throne's smooth arms—arms that had once been similarly gripped by Olaf's blood-stained, sausage-like fingers—and acknowledged this with a slight inclination of her head.

"You are welcome, Light Chaser. Although I confess

you are not as I had pictured you."

"Really, Highness? And may I be so bold as to ask how you'd imagined I might be?"

Gloriana brought a porcelain finger to her rosy lips. "I thought you'd be taller."

"I get that a lot."

"And we have this portrait." She waved to the wall where, surrounded by paintings of past rulers and legendary heroes, someone had hung a picture of an auburn-haired goddess. A chain of stars circled her head; golden threads made up her gown; and her features were arranged in an expression of divine contemplation. In one hand she held a memory collar; in the other a golden set of scales.

"Ah." Amahle placed the cat basket on the flagstones beside her and straightened up. The animal mewed piteously.

"Is this not a likeness of you?"

"I remember sitting for the preliminary sketches. The artist was a young man by the name of . . ." She clicked her fingers trying to summon the memory.

"Rothenburg," the queen said.

"Ah, yes." Amahle smiled. "Gregor Rothenburg. He was young and kind of attractive in a pallid, skinny way. And a little too free with his artistic licence, if I recall correctly."

"He was one of our greatest artists. A master. And because of his association with you, his surviving works are now considered treasures almost beyond price."

Amahle shrugged. As far as she was concerned, she'd spent a couple of weeks with Gregor, the protégé of another—probably now long-forgotten—artist. The young man had caught her eye during one of Olaf's interminable banquets, a soft-hearted contrast to the barbarians of the court. Thinking of him now, as a revered historical figure nine centuries dead, made her feel ancient and disconnected. How many decades had he lived, growing slowly old and infirm, after she'd returned to the stars? She was always curious about such things. She took lovers on many of the worlds she visited, and often wondered what became of them. Part of the delight of retracing her circuit was the prospect of being able to access the memories stored in their collars—assuming the collars had survived the intervening years; sometimes they got lost or damaged—and find out the missing portions of their stories. Did they marry, or pine endlessly for her return? Achieve greatness or live simple, unremarkable lives? It was a poignant experience, discovering what happened to them after she flew away, eternal and ageless, leaving them mired in the confines of whatever society had birthed them. Somehow, she felt such bittersweet knowledge kept her in touch with her humanity.

To change the subject, she congratulated Gloriana on her mastery of the Trade Language.

"Thank you," the queen replied. "I have been schooled in it since birth, in anticipation of your arrival."

"I appreciate the effort."

"You are welcome, although . . ."

"What now?"

"I'd assumed you might arrive with a little more pageantry."

Amahle shrugged. "I don't really go in for all that. I'm just here to do my job, that's all."

For the first time, the queen smiled, and her mask of formality slipped a notch. "As, dear Light Chaser, am I."

Amahle returned to her shuttle in the hills beyond town, where she had surreptitiously put down before the first light of dawn, and changed into something more befitting her legendary status. When she returned to the Keep, she had swapped her old dress for a black silk tunic with matching breeches, a gleaming steel breastplate, and a finely wrought scabbard containing a sword with a jewel-encrusted pommel. She felt faintly ridiculous but understood how important it was to project an image to impress the locals. After all, she'd need them to remember her again in another thousand years. And yet, she'd also been careful not to wear anything that might upstage the queen. She knew from experience that bad things happened when those in power felt their status threatened or diminished. Behind her, a train of cargo pods followed a metre above the rough ground, their motion through the air exactly the kind of casual, understated miracle she hoped might be verbally passed from generation to generation over the coming centuries.

The cat, she'd turned loose in the shuttle's cargo bay, hoping that with the help of some time to itself, along with the plate of sardines she'd procured from the food printer, it would acclimatise it to its new position as ship's cat.

When she reached the castle, Gloriana's servants set her up in the main hall, at a trestle table groaning with refreshments and sweetmeats. Amahle would have liked a cup of coffee, but given the nearest coffee plants were a dozen light years to antispinwards of this planet, she contented herself with a goblet of wine. While she drank, various ministers made speeches to the assembled crowd of nobles and dignitaries; trumpet blasts hailed proclamations of gratitude for her safe arrival; and minstrels played while everyone feasted. Then, protocols duly observed, they got down to business.

A thousand years earlier, Amahle had entrusted a hun-

dred memory collars to individuals all across Winterspite's sole habitable continent and left strict instructions
for those collars to be passed down through the generations, from old to young, until her next visit. To wear
one was an honour almost akin to a sacred duty, for when
the Light Chaser came back, she had let it be known she
would bring fabulous gifts in exchange for their safe return. After all, these collars were her primary reason for
being there—not that the locals knew that. She was careful to downplay the value of the collars in order to keep
their payment demands modest. But she'd gone through
this ritual on Winterspite at least eight times now, maybe
more. The *Mnemosyne*'s AI would know, if she could be
bothered to ask it. She was used to not knowing her deep
past; not even her enhanced neurones could recall everything. As new memories were made, so older ones vanished like exorcised ghosts to make room for them. At
every planet on her circuit, she collected in the old memory collars and distributed new ones to take their place,
rewarding the populace with luxuries, weapons, and gad-
gets that were exotic enough to be valued but not useful
enough to harm the stability of each world. The various
scattered societies of human space had been stable for
millennia, each locked into its own rigid status quo, and
it would be a serious offence to disrupt what had been
so carefully wrought during the Great Dispersal, when

those societies had been founded by the dynamic pioneers breaking free of Old Earth's restrictions and intolerance to establish their nirvana civilization out amid the stars. Although to her, some people's version of nirvana was weird indeed.

As well as the merchants who raced to the capital seeking profit, Gloriana quickly summoned the families who had been entrusted with collars on Amahle's last visit. When they stood nervously before her, they unclipped their collar—a thin, pearlescent band of pliable material—and handed it to her. In return, she presented them with a few trinkets and a new collar, along with a stern admonition to continue the tradition of handing it to their descendants. Out of the original hundred, nearly seventy collars came back. A disappointing total, but not unsurprising on a planet as brutal as Winterspite.

Many of those who sought an audience seemed awestruck to meet her in the flesh. She was, after all, a legend from ages past; a custom passed down in folk tales, art, and stories. Some, she was sure, had ceased actually believing in her and were now ashamed or stunned to see her before them. It was as if a powerful but partially forgotten deity had suddenly decided to drop by to see whether everyone still adhered to her commandments. Those who hadn't—whose families had lost, damaged or forgotten their collars—begged for mercy as they were hauled away by the palace guards to face the queen's displeasure for having deprived the world of the gifts the Light Chaser might have bestowed in return for their cooperation. Those who'd kept the faith presented their collars with expressions of palpable relief and smugness, accepting the tokens she handed them while they silently thanked every single one of their ancestors for not breaking the chain.

The process went on for a week as the collar wearers arrived, and the merchants offered what they considered riches. Amahle was more interested in handing out collars to the new batch of wearers, favourite sons and daughters of the queen's court presented in not-so-subtle fashion, as well as people Amahle chose at random—maintaining tradition. During this time, she tolerated the trades for material items the merchants believed valuable, a tactic which demonstrated her visit wasn't just about collars. So, incredibly complex medicines were given to sick children as if they were little more than a soothsayer's coloured water; a year's wages to the ragged and malnourished; handsome swords or daggers to the men- and women-at-arms; books and art to the scholars. Then, after a fortnight of godawful food and bitter wine and wearisome vigilance for the queen's erratic—and occasionally lethal—moods, she closed the last of the cargo pods and sat back in her chair with relief. She was seriously considering dropping Winterspite from her circuit, and to hell with her contract with EverLife. She was convinced Winterspite was becoming shabbier every time she visited. Or maybe she should just switch her trading to a more enlightened kingdom. *Yeah, right, so much choice there.* Her mood wasn't helped by the fact she hadn't got laid this visit. *Again: choices.*

As the guards hurried the last of the citizens out of the hall, Queen Gloriana swept back into the room. She had been absent since the midday feast, at which she'd picked sparingly at a piece of chicken while her noblemen and women gorged themselves around her.

"All done?" she asked.

Amahle gave the nearest pod a pat. "Yes, thank you, Your Highness."

"No, thank you, Light Chaser, for bestowing your favour on us once again. The payments you have made to our subjects will surely change many of their lives for the better and provide them with stories they shall doubtless use to regale their children and their children's children."

"You are quite welcome."

"And do you have anything in your magic boxes for us?"

Amahle smiled. "But of course. As you know, my collars are but inconsequential fripperies. Whims to gladden my ancient heart. But my real reason, as always, is to pay tribute to the royal bloodline of Winterspite, the most regal and divinely chosen monarch in all of creation."

Gloriana's cheeks reddened, and Amahle's smile widened. Flattery worked every time. She'd used the same words on Olaf the Butcher, and on each of his predecessors. She knew the script by rote. It was what the Light Chaser said before conferring her most special and valuable gifts.

"Behold!" She turned to the pod with a special gold emblem (hurriedly embossed) on the side, and pulled out a sequinned tunic.

"A shirt?"

"More than a shirt, your highness. The fabric of this garment contains useful properties. It can turn aside a dagger's thrust, a sword's strike, and even a bolt from the most powerful handheld crossbow. Whether you decide to keep it for yourself or hand it to your champion, it will make the wearer impervious to nearly all weaponry."

The queen's eyes narrowed as she considered the implications. "I see," she said. "A most valuable gift indeed."

"And of course, I've brought you emeralds and rubies." She slid a drawstring bag over the table. "Enough wealth to refurbish this whole town and introduce sanitation to the slum districts, should you see fit."

The queen weighed the bag in her hand. "Or to equip an army to subdue our neighbours to the north," she said.

Amahle shrugged. "I guess so."

"Thank you, Light Chaser. Will you be spending the night with us?"

Amahle glanced at the large window at the end of the hall. Darkness had fallen some hours ago.

"I guess so."

"Excellent." Gloriana smiled. "I shall have a chamber made up for you. But first—" She clapped her hands and a servant appeared carrying two glasses and a flask of brandy Amahle recognised as being one of the gifts she'd left Olaf the last time she'd been here. "First, we'll partake of this most ancient and venerable beverage, and you'll tell me something of your travels in the far distant lands beyond the sky."

III

WHEN AMAHLE RETURNED TO her shuttle in the grey dawn, the first thing she did was secure the cargo pods containing the used memory collars in the hold. As she snapped them into place, the cat came and rubbed its head against her shin.

"Hello." She bent down and tickled the purring creature behind its ears. "You liked the fish I made for you, did you?"

The cat followed her to the bridge.

"Good morning, ship," Amahle said brightly to the *Mnemosyne*'s AI, in orbit a thousand kilometres above. "Are we ready to go?"

"Already?" The ship's AI sounded surprised.

"You know I hate those medieval planets." Amahle unhooked her breastplate and let it fall to the deck with a loud clang. "There's shit everywhere." She kicked off her boots. Then she unhooked the scabbard and draped it over one of the control couches. "And sleeping on hay is a lot less romantic than it sounds." She scratched her stomach through her T-shirt. "Bloody fleas. I swear I got bitten at least three hundred times last night."

She gave the cat a sideways glance. The animal looked up at her uncomprehendingly. The AI said, "The feline has been cleansed of infestation."

"Really?" Amahle had an absurd mental image of one of the maintenance bots trying to force the uncooperative animal into a bath. "How did you manage that?"

"I employed nanobots to neutralise the parasites. The creature was unaware of the procedure."

"Nice." Amahle flopped into what was nominally her pilot's chair. She hadn't flown manually for . . . a century? She checked the screens to confirm the shuttle's status. All the displays were green. The cat jumped up into her lap and began to purr.

"I am currently using the same procedure on you."

"What?"

"Please try not to scratch too hard."

"Great," she muttered sullenly. "Have I had a cat before?"

"Several times."

"Oh. And . . . how did it work out?"

"They do not like freefall. They have to stay in *Mnemosyne*'s spin gravity areas."

"Okay."

"And you will have to train it to use a litter tray."

"Seriously? Me? What about a maintenance bot?"

"It's your pet. They respond best to human companionship. They do not respect my maintenance bots."

Amahle was sure she could hear disdain in the AI's voice. "All right. Take us back up to *Mnemosyne*."

The AI remote-piloted the shuttle on a fast ascent without noise or fuss. The little craft shone like a pearl as it emerged from the clouds into a bright, endless blue.

"Begin the primary drive start-up procedure," she said. "As soon as I'm aboard, I want to start the flight to Glisten."

"We'll be ready to leave orbit as soon as you dock," the AI replied.

She tried to summon up memories of the post-scarcity civilization where she was now headed. It was the end of the loop, where she could finally enjoy some civilized company before she set off yet again. There wouldn't be any mud or fleas there. The cat started to tense up as gravity dropped off, its claws digging a little deeper into her legs.

Below, Winterspite fell away like a duty discharged.

See you in a thousand years . . .

The time Amahle spent between the stars was hers to do with as she pleased. The *Mnemosyne* boasted an extensive library of electronic and print books, immersive entertainments, full-sense dramas, and even a good library of ancient movies from planets across The Domain, some from Old Earth itself. As well as its various opulent lounges, the life support section had a big gym, although she preferred her exercise in the swim aquarium with its shoals of natural and modified fish. And the AI could even be passable company when it made the effort—and she could be bothered to listen. However, her main source of entertainment came from the cargo of memory collars she collected from each world on the loop. Each of those precious collars contained ten centuries' worth of impressions and experiences. Her life might be spent alone voyaging between the stars, but she *lived* thousands of real lives. It was a perfect existence for someone of her kind.

She'd been forgotten, considered a myth, worshipped as a goddess, and forgotten again by the planets she visited on her eternal loop as their static civilizations carried on regardless. The lives of the planet-bound might have been nasty, brutish, and short by comparison, but the human experience she gained from the collars was uniquely enriching. So, she spent most of her time living vicariously through their recordings.

With Winterspite a dim point of light in her wake, and the *Mnemosyne* accelerating outwards from its sun at one gee, she went through the cargo pods to find the collar that had been assigned to Gregor Rothenburg. With her trophy swinging from a finger, she settled in the sunset lounge, a grandiose compartment currently formatted in homage to a millionaire's nineteen-sixties Malibu beach house. To match the elegant decadence, the AI produced a pitcher of margaritas. It was all part of the routine they'd developed. She started every new voyage checking up on her ex-lovers, to see how they'd fared once she'd left. She couldn't help but be curious how their lives had turned out. Had they married? Had they parlayed their notoriety as a Light Chaser's consort into wealth or political power?

She poured a drink from the pitcher and made herself comfortable in a recliner directly in front of the high windows looking out at the faux Pacific breakers. She studied the collar; sweat and grime of generations had indelibly stained the inside of the white band.

"You stay there," she said to the cat, which was perched on the arm of the chair. Her glance flicked down to the addermal strips on her thighs, which sealed the scratches that'd been inflicted during the shuttle's freefall approach to *Mnemosyne*. "Behave yourself while I see what we've got."

———————

As soon as Gregor woke that morning, he slung his patched and filthy nightgown around his shoulders. The flagstone floors of his studio were cold against his bare feet as he fought the urgent pressure in his bladder. He hurried to the back door, pulled it open, taking a long, steaming piss into the snow-covered yard. As he relieved himself, he sang a fragment of a half-remembered song.

Later, once he'd got the fire burning merrily in the grate and pulled on some decent woollen socks, he turned his attention to his easel. The picture he'd been working on was going to be a portrait of the Light Chaser Amahle—the goddess of the night sky, the immortal lantern-bearer of civilisation, and his own secret paramour. But so far, all he'd managed was a vague likeness. He found her eyes particularly tricky to get right. Only a week had passed since her departure, but every time he attempted to picture those miraculous eyes in his mind, they somehow blurred under his scrutiny, and the harder he concentrated, the more slippery the image became.

Gregor had often heard the wise men of the capital proclaim: We are all the sum and product of our memories. But if we start to forget little essential details—such as the exact likeness of a beloved—who then do we become?

As Amahle slipped from his mind's eye, he wondered if he was also losing a part of himself. As he saw it, the job of a painter was to salvage these little fading moments of time and preserve them on canvas, in order to remind us who we once *were and what was important to those people we used to be.*

And maybe even let them live again.

The marketplace philosophers claimed a person never really died as long as they were remembered. And that was the cause to which Gregor had dedicated his life: being remembered. He'd studied enough old masters to know it was a futile, quixotic defiance of implacable time. That given long enough, even paint dried and flaked. But if just one of his paintings managed to endure the next ten centuries intact, there'd be a chance Amahle would see it. A chance those same eyes giving him such trouble today would one day lay their gaze upon the cracked and faded image his fingers were crafting there this morning—and thus, in a small way, he would have bridged that almost unimaginable chasm of time in order to live once more in her memory, a thousand years hence.

It was a nice thought. On a more prosaic note, he also knew he had to get this picture completed by Friday if he wanted to keep his thumbs unbroken. It needed to be delivered to the main hall of the castle in time for the grand feast on Saturday evening, when King Olaf would celebrate the gifts and learning bequeathed by the Light Chaser and mark the start of the new millennial countdown until her next visit. And only a suicidal fool would risk displeasing Olaf the Butcher, a man so impatient, he had once had a chef boiled alive for being late with his breakfast. Gregor picked up his brush and chewed the end as he regarded his work in progress. Maybe it was the desire for posterity which was slowing him down? Perhaps a single canvas was unable to bear the weight of all that expectation?

He tried to focus on a clear memory of the Light Chaser, but all that came to mind were the sensations of lying with her—the feverish warmth of her skin; the wine on her breath; and the surprising strength that allowed her to pin him to the bed even as he thrust upwards into her.

How could that passionate intensity be conveyed in something as lifeless as paint? The only solution he could envisage would be to depict her as a goddess—to plunder the iconography of Winterspite's religious heritage in order to express his awe in terms a brute like Olaf might understand. A golden crown, he thought, or perhaps a set of justice scales? Something that places her both above and in judgement of mortal concerns. After all, kings died and castles fell, but the Light Chaser always endured, ageless and unending, in the dusk between the stars.

He dabbed his brush into some yellow paint and mixed it with a hint of white. Considered giving her one of those haloes that resembled a glowing space helmet.

A fist pounded against his door, dislodging dust motes to dance in the shafts of light squeezing through gaps in the warped planks. Cursing, he lowered the brush and waited, hoping whoever it was would go away. But the knocking started again, more insistently, and he sighed.

"All right, all right, I'm coming."

He shuffled across the stone floor in his socks and un-latched the door to find a young boy of perhaps ten years on the threshold, shivering in the snow.

"What do you want?" Cold air swirled in around Gregor's ankles. The flames in the hearth flickered as the logs spat.

Clear green eyes regarded him from a dirty, malnourished face. "Begging your pardon, sir. I have a message for the Light Chaser."

Gregor felt a flash of exasperation. "I'm afraid you're too late," he said. "She's gone."

The boy smiled, unruffled by his irritation. "But she will return, and when she does, she'll hear this message."

"What are you talking about, child?"

"Your collar, sir. It records all your experience, everything you see and hear and feel."

Gregor's paint-stained fingers reached up to touch the smooth band around his throat. For the first time, he realised his paintings might not be the only way to be remembered. That one day, in some unimaginably remote future, Amahle might experience this very moment through his eyes. The thought somehow terrified and comforted him.

"What's your message?" he asked gruffly.

The child smiled, and he rolled up his sleeve to expose a fresh tattoo—a string of eight numbers crudely etched into the reddened skin.

"My birth name is Bartz, but she will know me as Carloman; and I say this to her: You must not trust your AI." He nodded curtly and turned away.

Gregor watched the boy walk across the snowy ground, hugging himself against the chill. Exasperated, he called after him, "Is that it?"

Bartz or Carloman—whatever the boy was called—didn't stop or even look around. "For this time," he said. "Try and remember the last."

Amahle put the old memory collar on the arm of her chair and took a sip from her now-warm margarita.

"That was weird," she said.

"What was?" asked the ship's AI.

She nearly told it what she'd experienced, but something about that boy . . . Which was stupid. "Oh, nothing." She looked down at the cat, which had taken advantage of her distraction to curl up in her lap. Around her she sensed the familiar creaks and groans of the ship, the constant background hum of the negative mass drive carried through the great gantry spine, and the whisper of the air conditioning gusting inside the spacious chambers. The sounds were almost too faint and familiar to hear, but she had missed them while on Winterspite—along with the associated smells and tactile sensations that made the interior of the *Mnemosyne* her safe space and sanctuary. An egg from which she had no desire to hatch.

Still, something about the string of numerals on the boy's arm snagged at her mind. And that name: Carloman. It had a resonance for her, she was sure of it, although she had no idea how. She'd never met the boy, yet he claimed to know her. Impossible! Yet . . .

She shook her head in annoyance. The sensation of missing something so obvious was the same as a memory of a dream that had already faded. Though it was important, she was sure of it. Then there were the numbers. 10102159. They seemed familiar somehow. But why would a barbarian kid want to send her a string of numbers, knowing full well she wouldn't receive them until he'd been a thousand years dead? What possible relevance could such a code have for either of them? And that message: *You must not trust your AI.* That was just bullshit.

How can a kid from a thousand years ago, that I've never met, have such a disconcerting effect on me?

Amahle drained her glass and got to her feet, sending the cat stalking off across the lounge in a huff. "Can you show me some coordinates on Winterspite?" she asked the ship's AI.

The twilit Pacific Ocean outside the window vanished to be replaced by a three-dimensional projection of a globe.

"What are the coordinates?"

"10-10-21-59."

The globe flattened and expanded until Amahle was looking at a featureless stretch of slate-grey water.

"The middle of the southern polar ocean," the ship's AI reported.

Amahle frowned. "Are you sure?"

"If they are using standard format. Otherwise, I don't have sufficient data to extrapolate."

"Okay, never mind." She waved the projection away. Nobody on Winterspite would have ventured that far south. Their wooden sailing vessels simply weren't up to the hurricane-force winds that roared around the Southern Ocean. They'd be smashed to matchsticks before they got anywhere close. No, those numbers must represent something else.

Stellar coordinates? she mused. But it was unlikely anyone on the planet would have had the first clue about such things. The medieval stability of Winterspite was ruthlessly enforced by its savage rulers, who saw progress and democracy as a threat to their primacy. The only knowledge the planet's inhabitants had of the wider universe came from what they could see through their crude brass telescopes. Half of them thought she came from heaven rather than another world.

So, these numbers must mean something else. Something important enough for the kid to get them tattooed onto his arm. But what? Amahle drained her glass and refilled it from the pitcher. She looked down at the cat, who was now asleep on the pile of cushions it had commandeered for its bed. "What the hell was that?" she murmured.

IV

IT WAS TWENTY-THREE LIGHT YEARS from Winterspite to Glisten, and with *Mnemosyne* travelling at a fraction under lightspeed, relativistic time dilation meant Amahle would spend just over six years ship's time to complete the journey. Time enough to work through plenty of new memory collars and forget irrelevant anomalies.

Except...

10102159

She couldn't stop thinking about them. And... *You must not trust your AI.* How in all The Domain could some kid on Winterspite even know about an AI, let alone have an opinion on it? And if he did know about AIs, why would he have *that* opinion?

"Is something the matter?" the AI asked.

For a week as they accelerated away from Winterspite, she had sat in the Nordic lounge, a compartment textured to a cosy log cabin, with a fire burning eternally in the big stone chimney, and where snow swirled beyond the frosted-up windows. Except she'd switched the window to show Winterspite as viewed from the aft cameras, so now snowflakes drifted across the blue-white speck that had shrunk to an unremarkable star adrift amid the blackness of space. An arrangement which perfectly supported her melancholic mood.

She stirred irritably in the cosy old chair. "No, everything is lovely."

"Is that sarcasm?"

Amahle's expression changed, her features hardening. It reflected her change of attitude. There was nothing to be achieved by sitting around moodily waiting for an answer to magically appear. Those numbers meant something. She couldn't remember what, but that was okay, because old memories were always melting away to make room for the new; it was the price of living as long as she did. Her brain simply didn't have the capacity to retain thousands of years of life. But although the full memory had left, the essence of those numbers remained. So, they were important. Which meant they belonged in the past. Amahle stood up abruptly. *Try and remember the last.* She headed for the central lift.

"Are you looking for something?" the AI asked. "May I assist?"

She stalked along the neat racks lining the cargo compartment. "No." Stopped in front of the stack of pods that contained all the memory collars from Consensus, the cyber-moon that *Mnemosyne* had stopped at prior to Winterspite. A determined smile lifted her lips. *This might take a while.*

———————

Mnemosyne was four years into the flight to Glisten when Amahle found it: a single odd night in the memories of Zaro LDR, who belonged to the Methradx collective. They were a collective on the up when *Mnemosyne* had decelerated into orbit the previous circuit, which was why she'd chosen one of their members for a memory collar.

Consensus was one of the seventeen moons circling around Bacobia, a super-Jovian gas giant. Consensus had no atmosphere, but it did have an ocean of ice that covered the entire surface to a thickness of three kilometres, which formed a protective shell around a lower two-kilometre layer of liquid water, heated by volcanic vents. Some of the strangest aquatic creatures in the whole Domain swam through its ultra-black depths.

Mnemosyne dropped into a hundred-kilometre orbit amid the ring of zero-gee space factories and port stations owned by various collectives. Outside the starship's fluxfabrik shield, the moon was a jarringly white disk against Bacobia's ferocious pink and white and blue storm bands. Ice covered the globe from pole to pole, except for a single blemish twenty kilometres across, where an enormous mountain stood proud above the uniform frozen shell. *Mnemosyne's* sensors revealed the clutter of crystal domes covering the steep slopes. They were packed so tightly, like a smear of fish eggs, that very little of the black rock was visible: Jackeltown, the moon's sole settlement. The domes glowed a verdant green as artificial sunlight shone down on the swathe of terrestrial plants that covered the interiors. Tall, knife-blade towers rose from the rim of each dome, their varying heights producing an unsymmetrical crenulation.

"That layout is completely different from our last visit," the AI announced. "These domes are smaller and not quite circular, which allows for more of the mountain's surface to be covered."

Amahle nodded wisely. "And in comparison to our visit before that?"

"Different again."

As she studied at the image, she saw some of the domes were black, their crystal shells shattered in some recent skirmish. Vehicles and bots belonging to the victors moved through the gloomy, broken structures like scurrying ants. It was the way of Jackeltown, where the collectives clashed in arenas of commerce and mining and politics and good old-fashioned hit squads. A never-ending fight for alliances and survival and territory.

Small surface-to-orbit ships that had kept a respectable distance as the *Mnemosyne* braked into orbit now began to move in close. Dozens of comms masers splashed against the starship's silver fluxfabrik, welcoming Amahle, boasting their collective was the most powerful and useful, issuing invitations that promised all manner of extravagant parties and pleasures, politely querying what technologies she had brought to offer, declaring which of the memory collars had survived the intervening millennia and asking for favoured status among the descendants. The chatter was insistent and clearly not going to end.

"Print an avatar," she told the AI. "Let's get this over with."

No way was she going to risk going outside the ship's fluxfabrik shield, not to the ferocious and potentially lethal social Darwinism of Jackeltown, whose inhabitants could teach the tyrants of Winterspite a thing or two about treachery and mayhem.

The avatar produced in the medical bay's bioprinters was partly biological, partly cybernetic. It looked like her, moved like her, weighed the same, was capable of having sex, and could eat and taste food; but in addition, it had half a dozen weapon implants from primitive projectile guns up to a half-kiloton tactical fusion warhead—just in case negotiations took a really unpleasant turn. She walked it into an armoured non-atmospheric shuttle and flew down to the Methradx collective's cluster of domes.

Total time spent in Jackeltown: nine days. Information traded: molecular design for improved monomagnetic field generators, molecular design for improved anti-cancer nanites, molecular design for improved photon conductivity in fibre-optic cable, upgraded general analytic AI routines, and one small phial of alien biochemical toxin that Consensus had no cure for. Number of collective board members slept with for trade advantage: five (two so weirdly body-adapted, she was really glad she was avatar-riding). Number of memory collars exchanged in trades: fifty-eight. Number of memory collars received back: thirty-one (out of sixty-two issued on the last visit—their host families hadn't survived). One of the collars was from the LDR lineage; Zaro was the fourth member to wear the collar.

As soon as he stepped out of the lift, Zaro sent a legion of receptor drones to scout the corridors ahead. The airborne semi-bio bugs were flea-sized, equipped with multi-spectrum sensors; individually, they were almost insensate, unable to comprehend their environment, unresponsive to his com-

mands. *But together, the legion's conjoined processor cells boosted their ability almost up to semisentient class. Dozens of them flittered silently along the rock floor and cautiously swept the bundles of cables pinned to the curving wall. Overhead amid the roof's sculptured curves, they slithered up and down the ridges where the mining machines had cut their way through the original lava tube uncounted millennia before.*

Colourful data swarmed through his optical inserts. Neat columns of numbers and symbols, flowing at the upper end of human comprehension. In Zaro's case, he'd dosed up on respanix twenty minutes earlier when he left the Methradx dome, pushing his neurones to their biochemical limit. His hyped-up heart made the blood buzz through arteries, he was sure he could feel his brain heating up from the speed it was now working at. Analysis of the legion's data showed him clear corridors all around. He hurried forward, a movement akin to skittering, courtesy of his biocyber modifications. Right after his fifteenth birthday, his family paid for an arachlimb body-adapt; baseline ankles were replaced with a second knee joint, and a second shin grafted on below them ending in a cybernetic foot augment. Arms also had two sets of elbows each—

—Amahle grimaced in her comfortable chair. She always had trouble with cybernetically enhanced bodies, the unnatural nerve impulses from the bizarre extensions were hard for her neural structure to interpret—

—*so now Zaro possessed perfect mobility in the moon's 40 per cent standard-gravity field, especially down in the rat-hive of tunnels and shafts that riddled the solitary mountain. Feet on the floor, hands on the ceiling, toes and fingers gripped the tiniest ridges, allowing him to move with ease, the drone legion barely managing to keep ahead of him.*

The further he went, the more people he encountered; adepts like him and very unlike him, others who initially looked baseline—except when they came under scrutiny from the legion's sensors. Cyhumans in their life-support spheres. Everyone busy, busy . . . But then, the mines below Jackeltown were vital to its survival. The shafts provided access to the minerals necessary for the domes to flourish. Even now, after thousands of years of extraction, the strata were still thick and rich.

It took Zaro over an hour, but eventually he arrived at Break House, a big natural cavern the tunnelling machines had reached eight hundred years ago. These days, it was the centre of the district's life support systems, along with operations control, power station, maintenance shop, warehouse, hotels, bars, an arena, a couple of brothels, the clinic, commodities exchange, and several food marts. Lurking under the advertised commerce were suppliers of other goods, those that if you had to ask, your life expectancy shrank drastically. He made his way to the Nikoy bar, a cylindrical chamber made up of seven levels curving round a central fungus-jungle shaft bathed in violet light. The lower level, darker, noisier, and cheaper, was the one he'd been told to go to. As he arrived, he bumped some metü to amplify his muscle strength if a situation developed where the direct application of brute force would be needed. Somehow, its reaction with his biochemistry made his tongue go numb. His legion drones dispersed through the bar, tussling for position and bandwidth against a multitude of other legions and swarms and flocks and herds, comprising drones of varying sizes and ability. Down there, among the deals and the treachery, everyone was rightly paranoid.

He sat in a booth with the e-privacy screen open, waiting for the contact to make themselves known. A waitress with a marsupial pouch to keep bottles cold brought over a beer. Not her. Over on the stage, this hour's act took to the floor. A singer with an unwieldy string instrument that needed three of her four hands to produce a decent sound. Zaro thought she was kind of cute, with an extended neck flexing in time to the music. Her sinuous throat obviously contained adapted vocal cords, because she was singing both bass and soprano for a seriously heavy rock track. Her act was novel, Zaro decided, but not necessarily good.

The legion warned him a man was approaching the booth at an angle that put him out of direct line of sight/shot. A professional approach. The feed made him antsy. This was where it could all get physically unpleasant. The contact was supposed to be from a rival collective, selling geophysical mining data in exchange for entry into the Methradx collective. But it could be false flag, or double switch, or long-con infiltration, or even a counter recruitment aimed at Zaro himself. It was his job to try to find out before the shit hit the aircon.

The man wore black trunks and black sprinter shoes, showing off a baseline physique maybe ten per cent larger than a pureblood human. He was in his twenties, handsome, with steroid toning, and thick golden hair growing from his scalp and spine, groomed to a silky plume. But his eyes were the alterations that really caught Zaro's attention: perfect silver globes. Not even the drone legion scans could determine if they were bio or cytech.

"Hi," Zaro said, as the metü kindled a hot zinging along his blood vessels. Legion scan data was still coming up blanks. So, either the man was weaponless, or his tech was amazingly sophisticated. The only blemish on his dark-olive skin was a tattoo, reading: 10-10-21-59

"Hi yourself." Public dataflash provided an identity: Garvo DX. Which seemed to amuse him. "But you can call me Carloman. Pleased to meet you. Zaro, right?"

"Yeah."

"You're LDR family, currently under the umbrella of Methradx?" Carloman sat down opposite.

Zaro's face tightened in suspicion. "Yes."

"*The collar's the giveaway, in case you were wondering.*"

"*Okay.*" By sheer force of will, he stopped his hand going to the memory collar. The adornment was the LDR family's greatest honour, bestowing a prestige not dissimilar to a collective's executive class. When the Light Chaser returned to Consensus, she would give preferential trading terms to the collar wearers. Zaro switched on the booth's e-privacy shield, and then because he wasn't so naive to think the bar's management couldn't access it, he activated his own blocker.

"*Sorry.*" Carloman grinned with an amusement verging on mockery. "*I'm not your contact.*"

"*What?*"

"*But I do want to talk to you.*"

"*What?*"

"*We've probably got a few minutes until your actual contact shows up. So, what have you got to lose? You might even learn something.*"

"*Learn what?*" Zaro started to think Carloman's nonsense talk was a delay tactic while a bigger operation clicked into place subverting his goal. But the legion couldn't detect anything unusual in the bar. Yet.

"*Your vocabulary is kinda limited, isn't it?*" Carloman said.

"*What?*"

"*Okay. One conversation. I'll pay for your time.*" Some-

how, those tight trunks hid a pocket. A two-centimetre cube of pure platinum was produced and placed on the table next to Zaro's beer.

"What the hell is this?" Zaro tried to guess if Carloman was some kind of hooker. If so, his pickup technique was the strangest. "Look, friend, I don't know what you want, but I'm not buying."

"You think you're not. But that's a matter of perception."

"Wha . . . Seriously, I'm waiting for someone."

"I know. But that's reality for you: perception. You perceive you're waiting for someone. In this reality, I'm a stranger telling you a story. In another, I could be the contact or an assassin or a pusher, or maybe you're the defector and I'm the contact."

"That's what you're trying to tell me, you're from an alternate universe? Were we friends there?"

"Appreciate your good humour. But no, there is no alternative universe, there is only this one. But how we perceive it, well, that's the problem. Turns out reality isn't as stable as you think. And by think, I mean hope."

Zaro was starting to slide round to the possibility that Carloman was nothing more than someone tripping a little too high. Ordinarily, that would be interesting, fun, even, but not here and now. And not with the e-shield closed and the contact unable to see him. "I don't have a problem with how I perceive things. Except maybe you. I'd like you to vanish from my perception altogether. Okay?"

"What do you think reality is for?"

"Wh . . . Excuse me?"

"Why are we here? Why does the universe exist?"

"I am not joining your religion."

"We live for the experience life gives us. It enriches our soul, allowing us to grow and mature every time we reincarnate."

"Reincarnate? Oh, come on—"

"Reincarnate," Carloman said compellingly. "That, Zaro, is the purpose of this universe, to give our life a home. Which, as a wise man once said, is not only queerer than we suppose but queerer than we can suppose; and also: that it is immensely unlikely that mind is a mere by-product of matter."

Zaro wanted to tell Carloman to piss off, like Right Now, but he was trapped by being unable to cause a scene, something that would scare off the real contact. "If reality is all about perception, then why am I perceiving you? I don't want to."

"Because there are rules. They can't be broken, but they can be played. I want you to remember that. And you know who I mean by you."

"Sure. No problem."

"Good. Because we're being played. All of us. Right now. This reality, our reality, is not the original reality we encountered when our souls first emerged into it from our holm be-

yond. The physical universe remains a constant, of course. But our perception of it has been manipulated, our destiny has been taken from us. And we don't know it."

"You seem to know."

"Yes." Carloman stared at him with those unnatural silver orbs, a stare that cut right into Zaro—almost as if he were studying something lurking within. Judging. "Some of us do. And you can be one of them, if you can just remember. Or, at least, trust me."

"Me?"

Carloman smiled enigmatically. "You know I'm talking to you. Again . . ."

"So, we're all being manipulated?"

"Yes. I don't know who they are. Call them The Exalted, if you like, because they have some kind of advantage over us. They found us somehow, found the time we exist in this universe, and they're using their knowledge to block us."

"Block us? From what?"

"From growing. They're stunting our spiritual growth by manipulating the timeline to make sure it never deviates from this abomination of reality."

"You're crazy. The Domain is the pinnacle of our species. We're interstellar! We live on so many planets, we don't even know the true number. That makes our species practically immortal. We're immune to Armageddon."

"Yes. But only in this form. Every world"—again the

forceful stare—"*you fly to on your everlasting circuit is static.
They don't change. Every. Single. World. There is no progress
anymore, not on any level: social, technological . . . Why?*"

"That is bullshit. Look around you, we're so far ahead of
the medieval worlds, they'd think we're gods if they ever came
here."

"Yeah. So, why hasn't Jackeltown ever expanded? There
are a dozen other moons orbiting Bacobia alone. Then there
are three solid worlds in this star system. Why haven't we ter-
raformed them?"

"None of them are suitable."

"Wrong. They are all suitable. They're just difficult."

"There! You said it. Terraforming is too difficult. We can't
afford it."

"Yes, because somehow Jackeltown society is locked into
this specific economic structure. Consensus never changes, no
matter which collective is on the up. If one collective ever gets
too big, big enough, say, to start investing in a project like
terraforming another planet, the others become so worried
about its power, they ally to bring it down."

Zaro gave a bitter laugh. "The way of the world, pal."

"The way of every world. Every inhabited planet in The
Domain has a society designed for one thing: stability. Ask
yourself, Why? Who does that benefit?"

"We had unstable societies back on pre-starflight Earth.
All it brought was misery and wars. You want to go back to

that era?"

"No. I want to advance past this one. I want us to grow again. The human spirit is capable of such wonder if only it is free to soar."

"So, that's it, you're an anarchist?"

"No. I'm a liberator. I want to destroy The Exalted. It's the only way to be sure."

"You want a war? You're not an anarchist, you're worse: you're a recidivist. We've left all that behind."

"Tell that to the billion people a year who die needlessly on the medieval worlds, drowning in pain and shit. Their lives here have become pointless. I'm going to save them. With your help."

"Me!"

"Amahle."

"Oh, fuck, you think you're talking to her."

"You think I'm not?"

"You're crazy."

"Agreed: from your perception. And that's what we need to change. Amahle, I swear to you we've met before, not just in previous incarnations among other realities but in this one, too. And we're going to meet again, because that's our destiny. You just have to remember me. I know it's difficult, but I know you can do that. It's part of your gift from the holm, like mine. Just . . . wake up. And find me."

"What?" Zaro dropped out of his tolerance zone and

started to worry. This maniac was effortlessly taking up too much time, endangering his actual meeting. He wondered if he should just use a weapons implant and blow Carloman straight to hell.

But Carloman's grin was insultingly superior, as if he could divine those very thoughts. "Sorry, nothing personal. I'm being preachy for her, not you. Sweetheart, you have to remember me, that's the way to remembering what you are, the gift we share. It'll set you free. It'll set everybody free."

Zaro put on his tough-guy face. "Leave. Now. First and only warning."

"Sure thing."

And the weirdo was gone, shimmering through the screens and blockers, leaving Zaro to stare at the empty booth in be-wilderment. It had to be some kind of play by another collective, they wanted to mess with his head. "No, you fucking don't," he grunted. He bumped another respanix, and to fuck with the dosage consequences. His mind locked into perfect focus. And in reward, that was the moment his contact arrived. The true game began. This shit was what he lived for.

———

Amahle removed the collar, her thoughts in a daze. What she'd just experienced wasn't possible. The same person on a different world, centuries and light years from the other collar memory of him? Not physically the same, this Carloman was nothing like the boy child on Winterspite. Only the name was the same.

And the attitude. The charisma.

A charisma which she could not banish, because even the boy had held her attention. A charisma which was now becoming something of an obsession. There was no way Carloman could exist the way he said he did. Unless. . . . Unless he was telling the truth. But even if he was, how did he travel about like this? It was as if he'd become a ghost, flitting between worlds to haunt her.

A holm beyond the universe? Reincarnation?

"No way," she whispered.

"I have prepared your evening meal for you," the AI said. "Fillet steak medium rare, just as you like it. And skinny fries, of course."

"Put it in a sandwich," she told it. "I'm going to collarbinge."

V

AFTER A YEAR OF smooth deceleration, the *Mnemosyne* eased its way into the Glisten system. Smaller craft buzzed around it: curious onlookers come to see the arrival of a Light Chaser at the end of its loop. Maybe even a news crew or two—although the millennial comings and goings of the various Light Chasers on their respective circuits had ceased to be strictly newsworthy aeons before. More of a curiosity these days, like the seasonal migration of birds or whales, or the long slow cycle of a comet.

That's what I am, Amahle thought: *a comet. A frozen wanderer sidling in from the darkness to briefly warm myself by the light of the sun, before being flung back out on the next lap of my long, solitary orbit . . .*

She watched her screens as the *Mnemosyne* slid into a cavernous, four-kilometre-long maintenance bay in the orbital docks the size of a Mars moon. Then, securely held in place by invisible fields, the great old ship powered down its systems for the first time in a thousand years.

Amahle could have sworn she heard the ship's AI sigh contentedly, like a man taking off his boots after a long hike, though the sound could equally have been caused by the air pressure in the cabin adjusting itself to match that of the station.

A docking tube extended out from the bay wall and clamped over the main airlock. Amahle had dressed for the occasion, in an outfit incorporating fashionable and traditional clothing from each of the worlds she'd visited. She had the shiny breastplate she'd worn on Winterspite, over which she'd slipped an ankle-length dark red great-coat with epaulets and military brocade. She'd pulled her hair back and pinned it in place with chopsticks and eagle feathers, and a single jewelled braid hung from her left temple, brushing her cheek. Her synthetic squid-skin boots rippled with explosions of colour each time she took a step.

"Pretty badass," she said approvingly, checking her reflection one final time. Then she made her way along the docking tube into the habitable parts of the station, carrying the elderly cat in its basket. The dear old thing was in poor shape now, overweight, incontinent, and nearly blind. She'd never expected it to last this long, but being pampered on a starship with a lower gravity than its birth world was clearly the perfect milieu for felines.

Glisten's ancient orbital dock was a nation unto itself,

housing millions of permanent residents alongside a more transient population of travellers and tourists. Its foundations had been constructed in the first decades following the Great Dispersal. Since then, it had accreted additional modules, old starships, industrial installations, and a hundred other extensions, until it resembled a roughly spherical coral reef a thousand kilometres across. Newer technologies had been plated over older structures. In its corridors, the air smelled of peaches. The controlling AI monitored the temperature to make sure it was always optimum for each individual's comfort, and the floors had a subtle springiness that made walking on them a pleasure.

I'm home, Amahle thought, but she didn't feel it. Not really. Not inside, where it mattered. *So, was I born here?* There were times when her constant ablation of old memories was deeply annoying.

A representative from the EverLife consortium waited for her. The man was bald and blue-skinned, wearing a neatly tailored business suit. He introduced himself as Dravian and took her to a busy café overlooking the bay that held her ship, constantly glancing over his shoulder at the small cargo bot which trundled loyally after her, carrying the collars she'd acquired on the loop.

"Welcome back, Captain," he said. "I trust your circuit was successful?"

Looking around, Amahle saw other bald, blue-skinned individuals in the crowds moving along the concourse and decided Dravian's artificial hues must be a fad. As fashions went, she'd seen worse.

"Collars collected as specified in the contract," she told him, and gestured at the cargo bot. "Eighty-two per cent of the ones I issued."

"Ah, that's disappointing," Dravian said diplomatically.

"Not really. Some of the worlds on my loop are really quite savage. Life expectancy is not great. Which is why Glisten enjoys them so much, I expect. A naughty but safe experience for the more jaded among your population. Am I right?" She knew she was, because that was the nature of Glisten. It was just her AI that gave her cause for concern.

You must not trust your AI.

It had been curious why she hadn't loaded all the collars into the cargo bot before disembarking.

"I haven't finished with them," she told it as she shut the bot's last container, leaving the fifty collars she'd selected still in their original containers. "There's a few I still want to experience."

"But you will soon have more," it said.

"On-board flight time from here to Reatinala is eight years. There are only so many dramas I can immerse myself in."

"I understand."

It hadn't put up any further objections. Now she waited to see if it had exposed her breach of contract to EverLife.

"You know us very well," Dravian said with a smile that revealed perfect white teeth, his gaze slipped to the cat sleeping in its basket, and for the briefest moment his composure flickered. "Eighty-two per cent is well within the contract provision. I'll authorise the dock to begin *Mnemosyne*'s refit immediately."

"I should hope so." The *Mnemosyne*'s engineering section could fabricate a vast catalogue of components should any of the on-board systems fail during a flight, but it didn't quite have full von Neumann levels of self-replication. In the past, she'd idly wondered if that was to force her to return to Glisten at the end of each circuit, where the facilities for a full refit for the drive and generators were to be found. Now it didn't seem quite so fanciful. In fact, *sinister* was a description she was considering applying.

"And you'll authorise a new loop contract with EverLife?"

She could sense the anxiety behind his cool blue façade. "I believe I will."

"Thank you."

The table dispensed two steaming bowls of something

that looked and smelled like yellow pus. Amahle wrinkled her nose. The last time she'd been on Glisten, the station had been undergoing a nostalgic craze for traditional Chinese and Nepalese cuisine, and she'd been kind of hoping to be presented with some yak-meat mómo, or at least a decent pào mó.

"And in the meantime," Dravian continued, "the collars you have collected on this trip will be entered into our collection, along with the millions of others you and your colleagues have obtained over the millennia, and thus be made available for the edification and enjoyment of our customers."

Amahle stirred the gloop in her bowl. She didn't much care what happened to the recordings, as long as she got paid for them. In an age in which few people ever travelled between the stars, the collars were a way for Glisten's population to vicariously experience the diversity of human civilisation. Loaded into the planet's data net, they would be made available to anyone who wished to immerse themselves in other lives and other cultures.

Dravian put his fingers to the base of his throat. "And we still can't convince you to wear a collar yourself? There are those among the population who would pay handsomely to live the life of a starship pilot."

"I'm afraid not." Amahle put her hands in the pockets of her greatcoat and placed her left ankle on her right knee. The squid boots shimmered. "I prefer to keep my thoughts private."

Dravian raised a condescending eyebrow. He smiled. "Doesn't that make you a hypocrite?"

"Fuck you." Amahle felt her cheeks redden.

"But it does, though, doesn't it?"

"So what if it does?" She leaned back. "I don't care what you think, Dave or whatever your name is." Her voice was as cold and unforgiving as interstellar space. "Your opinion doesn't matter to me. The next time I come back here, I'll be dealing with someone else. You'll be dead and gone, and even *I* will have forgotten who you were."

Heads turned. Taken aback, Dravian smiled weakly.

"I'm sorry," he said. "I meant no offence."

"Yes, you did." Amahle narrowed her eyes. "You were trying to put me on the defensive. But I spend my life making deals. I've gone toe-to-toe with business leaders, warlords, and royalty. And more than that, I'm a woman. I know when someone's trying to neg me into something I don't want to do."

"I was not . . ."

"Yes, you most definitely were." She pulled the flap of her coat back to reveal the dagger at her hip. "And you should know the last man who tried to insult me into bed now sings soprano."

Dravian raised cobalt hands in alarm. "I was *not* trying to seduce you."

"Damn right you weren't." Amahle took hold of the cat basket and stood. Her chair legs squeaked against the floor. She drew herself up to her full height. "Let's just remember who's the immortal space goddess around here, shall we?"

———————

While the ship was being refitted, Amahle stayed in a dockside hotel suite. It was smaller and less luxurious than the lounges on board *Mnemosyne,* but she didn't care. It was *different.* The cat stayed with her. It habitually peed in its basket, poor thing. Thankfully, the basket's smart-fabric cushioning neutralised the smell before it bothered her nostrils.

In the evenings, she broke with tradition and spent her time in the room instead of visiting the renowned restaurants along the station's main promenades, which promised delicacies from a hundred worlds, cooked directly from the chefs' collar memories. Somehow, her mood just wasn't right to socialise. *You must not trust your AI.* Damn that kid! *Him . . .*

Nobody seemed to be upset by her self-seclusion. Her status as a Light Chaser gave her a certain cachet among the locals, but they were used to her kind. Even though she hadn't been back there in a thousand years, other Light Chasers had recently come and gone. Their loops brought them back there at varying intervals, meaning Glisten saw several dozen every century.

That left her free to prop herself up on the hotel bed, surrounded by half-eaten dishes ordered from those renowned restaurants, contemplating the riddle which had come to dominate her every waking minute. Ironically and infuriatingly for someone who could apparently move freely across centuries and planets, Carloman hadn't appeared in any of the hundred and thirty-five collar memories she'd reviewed in the last two years since accessing Zaro's memory. So, once more, she closed her eyes, running first Gregor, then Zaro's memory. Living the two scenes as if they were happening in real time.

As the child to Gregor: *Try and remember.*

Then: *We're going to meet again,* he'd told Zaro.

And craziest of all: *Reincarnation.*

As if he'd got some kind of messiah complex. But then he'd appeared twice to her, as different people on different worlds in different centuries. The only thing—*only*—that might explain such an impossibility was another Light Chaser playing some ridiculous game with her. But even that didn't make any kind of sense. If she knew any of them, she'd forgotten centuries ago. *Could that be the reason? He's angry because I moved on, or spurned him?*

She screwed up her face. Carloman had seemed so sure in both—*damnit!*—incarnations. And there was no doubt he was talking directly to her, and not for the first time. But when had they originally met, and what did that number mean?

When . . .

"Holy shit!" She sat bolt upright, scattering plates and causing the ancient cat to raise its head from the basket and peer in her direction with its rheumy eyes. 10102159. It wasn't a set of coordinates; it was a *date*.

10-10-2159.

The tenth of October 2159.

She told the hotel's network to connect her to Glisten's AI. *You must not trust your AI.* "What's the date," she asked it, "in the old Earth calendar?"

"Today is the twenty-first of May 28367."

So, over twenty-six thousand years ago . . .

"How old am I, in Earth years?"

"Twenty-six thousand, three hundred and fifty-five."

Amahle performed some quick mental arithmetic, not easy when you had to take relativistic time compression into account. "So, I would have been a hundred and forty-seven in 2159?"

"Correct."

"That can't be a coincidence."

"What can't?"

"Do you have any information on my whereabouts in 2159?"

"The personnel file EverLife holds on you begins in January 2160, which is when you joined the Light Chaser programme. Before that, you were on Earth."

Amahle bit her lip. Carloman had warned her not to trust *Mnemosyne*'s AI. So, presumably, that included all AIs. But right now, the network was her only source of reliable information.

"Does my file contain the name Carloman?"

"Yes."

She felt her heart quicken. "Who is he?"

"He was your husband."

Shit! "Did he join the Light Chaser programme with me?"

"No. Your husband died the year before."

"A year . . . You mean in 2159?"

"Yes."

"When? What date? Exactly!"

"October the tenth."

———————

Amahle took a shower, standing there for an age to let the hot water stream over her head, running down her face until it washed away her tears.

She was being stupid.

And yet . . .

Wrapped in a thick white robe, she curled in the bed with the sleeping cat wheezing at her feet. Her hair was wrapped in a towel. Her skin tingled from the scalding water. And right then, she felt the void in her chest. The deep, melancholy ache that had never been filled. An urge that could not be satisfied by any number of casual romantic encounters—the desperate, suppressed craving for the companionship of an equal. For a face that would persist for more than a few days. A life that would touch her for more than a few sweaty hours on a distant planet. Sometimes, being alone and detached from the ongoing sweep of human history was a privilege almost too painful to bear. But had that void in her soul been grief all this time?

When she woke up, the cat was dead.

Ten days later, the newly refurbished *Mnemosyne* eased its way out of the vast maintenance bay and powered away from the orbital docks. In its cargo holds were crates of brand-new memory collars from EverLife, along with carefully selected trade goods Amahle had picked from the medinas around the edge of the port, where local merchants hawked trinkets, curiosities, and artworks gathered by other Light Chasers on their circuits.

As Glisten fell away astern, Amahle retired to her private cabin, where, sitting on a pile of silk cushions, she began reviewing the collars she had saved from her last circuit. A month later, she found Carloman's next message.

In this incarnation—yes, *incarnation*! She didn't believe it, obviously, not holms beyond the universe and souls and reincarnation. Such utter bullshit. But to analyse and expose whoever (whatever) this sprite-like entity was, this entity who'd maliciously claimed her dead husband's name, she had to have some framework to attach events to. His lie was the simplest.

Okay, so . . . in this recording, he was a very old man, with thinning white hair and mottled skin stretched over a hunched and frail skeleton. He wore a grubby toga that exposed the deeply wrinkled skin of both arms, exposing a tattoo: 10-10-2159. Those same arms which shook as he supported himself with a gnarled walking stick. Life had been hard to him, but his eyes still burned with determination.

"Go to Pastoria," he insisted in a dry, whispery voice. "Make me a strangelet."

Amahle frowned. Pastoria was one of the planets on

her circuit, but she wasn't due there for six hundred years. She couldn't break the cycle. It would throw everything off. The routine she'd established across millennia would be ruined. Whole populations would wait their entire lives in vain for her expected return. And anyway, Pastoria had no technology above a cart wheel. So, why . . . Her eyes opened wide in realization.

"Damn it, yes, of course," she grunted.

The AI responded to her voice. "Is something wrong?"

"No." She stretched out on the silk pillows and glared at the ceiling.

"You sound annoyed."

"I'm fine."

"So, there's nothing I can help you with?"

Amahle laced her fingers behind her head. "What's a strangelet?"

"I'm sorry, that information is classified."

Amahle frowned, the AI had never denied her any information before—not that she could remember, anyway. *You must not trust your AI* . . . "Classified? Why?"

"The information has weapon applications. Under the terms of the Domain Charter, it is only available to democratic governments."

"Oh, okay." She didn't believe that for a second.

Over the next two days, Amahle reviewed Carloman's three messages and, to her dismayed surprise, found she was starting to believe what he was telling her. She had no choice. Nobody could have coordinated a deception of such magnitude across such vast gulfs of time and space. It would be impossible—and, as one of her ancestors had been fond of quoting, once you eliminated the impossible, what remained had to be the truth. If someone on Winterspite had told her such a tale, she would have dismissed it as superstitious nonsense. But now, having put together everything Carloman had told her from encounters, she had no choice but to believe he really was her dead husband, stalking her through his various incarnations as she remained ageless and difficult to reach. And that reality and human destiny were being manipulated by mysterious beings for their own inscrutable ends.

"What a headfuck," she declared.

She stood up and paced around her sleeping quarters, not liking where this train of thought was taking her—because if she believed what Carloman had told her, she also had to believe his warning not to trust the *Mnemosyne*'s AI. But that was like asking a planet-dweller to stop trusting in gravity. To stop trusting that the sun would come up in the morning. The AI had been a constant presence in her life. For thousands of years, it had run this ancient, colossal ship in partnership with her and provided her only company between worlds. She had always trusted it implicitly. It had never occurred to her to do otherwise. AIs ran everything—transport capsules, city power grids, global economies . . . They always had and they always would. They were responsible for the peace and stability of the past twenty-six thousand years since the Great Dispersal. To question their trustworthiness was to call into doubt the very bedrock of human civilisation. It was unthinkable.

And yet . . .

Why had her AI refused to explain what a strangelet was? The excuse about weapons was something a five-year-old would come up with. It couldn't be a coincidence that the one thing Carloman wanted her to build was also the first and only thing the AI had ever refused to explain.

Classified, my arse!

Once upon a time, she would have known all about strangelets, she was sure. But that was the bane of immortal existence. The past was forever lost behind you. She could press the AI for details, but there had to be a level of enquiry that was a tipping point, alerting it to take action against her insurrection.

She knew it had the capability to edit her memories, a treatment it had used in the past during medical recovery procedures. There were log files about violent personal encounters on the more backwards worlds. Four thousand years before, Gothbal had been dropped from her circuit completely, she'd never been back—the only log entry was: *emergency surgery to reattach leg, post-trauma memory deletion, assault stress disorder alleviated.*

But what if the AI cured more than PTSD? What if the loss of her deep history wasn't simply down to old age alone? What if the machine had been regularly deleting anything that might disrupt her mission, seeking to preserve the status quo the way its brethren preserved the stability of human society across the galaxy? Perhaps this wasn't the first time Carloman had tried to contact her. Perhaps she'd rebelled before and all trace of that insubordination had been purged from her mind.

Suddenly, she felt very alone. If she couldn't trust her AI, she couldn't count on it to take her where she wanted to go, specifically Pastoria. If it insisted on following its preordained schedule, could she stop it? For all she knew, it might simply reset her brain the next time she submitted herself for the routine gene therapy she underwent every couple of decades to reverse cellular senescence, scouring away all trace of anything not relevant to her assigned role. She hugged herself and left her quarters. For the first time, the *Mnemosyne* had begun to feel less like a refuge and more like a cage.

Unbearably frustrated, Amahle walked down to the deck that housed the swim aquarium, where she stripped off and immersed herself in the warm waters. As she floated on her back, she began to feel the tension soothe out of her neck and shoulders. Her hair floated free, forming a halo around her head, and only her face remained above the surface—as if she were some aquatic creature pushing its face into another realm.

She closed her eyes and let her thoughts drift. *Remembering me is the key,* Carloman had said. But no human mind could hold thousands of years of memories, she'd always known and accepted that, presumably it was how she'd been able to sign up for the Light Chaser programme in the first place. Her life would always be anchored in the unending now. Yes, Carloman could remember. *Our gift,* he'd called it.

That notion produced a faint resonance amid her unfocussed mind.

Our gift.

He'd smiled as they'd stood on the ancient stone wharf of a Sicilian fishing village, holding hands and looking into each other's eyes. Joyful that now the third Italian War of Independence was over, they'd found each other again. As always.

Amahle sat up fast, sending ripples racing out over the surface of the swim aquarium. And that wonderous glimpse of the far past didn't fade. Her memory from the nineteenth century burned as brightly now as it had when it was happening in real-time. "We found each other," she whispered incredulously. "We always do."

"Found what?" the AI asked.

"Nothing." She sank back into the water, smiling to herself. And where there was that memory... others came rising like ghostly tendrils out of some part of her mind that existed beyond the purely physical, somewhere that the rejuvenations and edits of the ship's medical suite could never reach. The holm, where her soul originated from, occupying the non-realm outside spacetime; both separate but still existing within the overall cosmos. Together, the two intersected, a contact which created the miracle that was the mind, animating flesh, delivering purpose to otherwise insensate clusters of mere organic chemistry.

The holm was many—all—and also one. It had sensed potential in the complexity of the beasts evolving on primordial Earth and pushed its way in through the barrier between its dimension and the physical universe. Its myriad strands knew space and time, tasting light and heat and experience for the first time, experience which allowed them to evolve as the souls of the crude planetbound creatures.

Oh, their bodies died, as was the way with all of the universe's frail biology, but when they did, the souls reached back in to occupy new growth, knowing the wonder of physical reality again and again. Ordinarily, they didn't carry past lives with them when they returned, allowing each life to be fresh, venerating what they underwent to the fullest extent. Some did, though—a gift, or curse.

But their holm wasn't the only one out there in the null-folds of the cosmos. Other holms sought experience within the beauty of spacetime. And one, The Exalted, had found a way to increase the experience which enriched them, by feeding on human experience like vampires of the mind.

Amahle stared up at the compartment's ceiling, her jaw muscles hardening as she rediscovered the knowledge that had been concealed for millennia. Carloman was right, The Exalted were the ultimate enemy. And if he needed a strangelet to defeat them, then that was what she would bring him.

VI

OVER THE NEXT FEW days, she began to make sense of
the memories that came oozing back into her consciousness. She'd lived so many times, many of them with Carloman, but not all. Vistas from history roamed behind
her eyes, the many reincarnations that never obeyed a
linear order. Her extrusion into history jumped about
at random, from the numbing horror of the mid-twenti-
eth century to the Holy Roman era, Renaissance Europe
to the Incan Empire, then back to early eighteenth-cen-
tury China; a jumble of enriched events; she'd lived short
lives, lives without love, lives full of joy, some even over-
lapped, for souls didn't emerge from a place that obeyed
the physical universe's steady temporal progress. Those
unknowingly shared lives allowed her to witness the
world from both ends of society at the same time, the suf-
fering and the effortless material comfort of wealth. The
inequality and the achievements, the astonishing range
of beliefs and expectations. Becoming a human provided
an endless variety that every soul coveted.

It was that very triumph of people and their differences, she realised, that made them so desirable to The Exalted, who must be creatures with a much more limited physical engagement with their environment. Try as she might, she couldn't imagine what their biological bodies must be like to produce such a bland passage through life.

Bland but smart. Their painful banality had inspired them to steal from human souls what their own existence could never provide.

Now she knew the truth, she was ready to fight. Carloman would know how to deal with the ship's AI, she was sure about that. Somewhere, somewhen, he'd have told her. So, she continued to play her Light Chaser role to the full and started to binge on memory collars. It was reasonable-enough behaviour, she'd kept her little stash back from EverLife for exactly this reason, and she still missed the cat. What else was a girl supposed to do?

Seven collars, passed down through the families anointed with privilege by the Light Chaser, lives to be preserved for eternity and revered by the godlike inhabitants of Glisten. In reality, cheap entertainment for the jaundiced lives of a world with no strife, whose endless leisure was as much a curse as the short, often-brutal lives they accessed so eagerly. Generations of memories as the collars went from the dying to the newborn again and again, until the moment the Light Chaser came and removed the collar like a coronation in reverse.

Looking at it like that triggered a huge pang of guilt. The way she'd lived on the *Mnemosyne* was a small, pathetic copy of The Exalted; incapable of fulfilling herself, she lived through others alone.

The lives contained in seven collars reviewed, seven multiple generations of each family. Then she put on the eighth collar.

It belonged to the Monray family on Farshire: good people, hard workers from a village on the Rothensay estate, their trade with the Light Chaser leveraged astutely.

Amahle remembered Farshire well enough. A world of subtle apartheid, always easy to ignore because there, difference was buried in the genes not in display through ethnicity, and she had far more in common with the landowner families than the rest of the population.

She'd landed just outside Beckett, the capital, two hundred years before her trip to Winterspite. The aerodrome was just a wide, grassy parkland with a cedar-lined greenway leading across the wolds to the city. It existed solely for her shuttlecraft; Farshire didn't have aircraft. The most advanced vehicles there were steam trains.

It was raining when the shuttle touched down. An official welcome committee was waiting for her under a hastily erected marquee. Farshire didn't have radio communication, but there were telescopes and binoculars.

The *Mnemosyne* decelerating into orbit was easy enough to see.

She had spent months selecting her wardrobe for the visit. Farshire was always a lovely holiday, stress-free, especially as Winterspite loomed in her future like some dour penance. So, old classic dresses were examined, new ones printed; ball gowns, pencil skirt suits, jackets with a hundred buttons, high collars, scandalous décolletage, wide skirts plumped by lace petticoats, leather boots, gorgeously impractical shoes, heels! And hats—tall, wide, small, ridiculously big, coquettish; with veils, with flowers, feathers, *fruit*. It was dress-up party time again, revisiting a youth she could never quite remember, except from the delight such juvenility awoke.

To disembark, she chose an ankle-length suede skirt and formal black jacket, worn under a scarlet coat with exuberant shoulder pads, and a double row of silver buttons all the way down the front that gleamed even under the rumbling grey clouds. The outfit was topped off by a deep-purple velvet bowler hat—rakish angle, of course.

Earl Jlbana, Beckett's lord mayor, stood at the bottom of the shuttle's door ramp, his top hat and tailcoat immaculate, solid gold chain of office so thick and heavy, it looked like it might topple him over. He bowed deeply. "Light Chaser, we are honoured by your visit. Welcome to our world and its jewel: Beckett. I hope your time here fulfils every expectation. If there is anything you need, my office is at your disposal, day and night."

Amahle held out a gloved hand, which he kissed. "You are too kind, Lord Mayor. This is why I always look forward to coming back to Farshire, it is the prize of my circuit."

Four jet black horses pulled the big carriage they rode in down the greenway to the city. Once they were over the bridge, they slowed down so people could catch a glimpse of the fabled Light Chaser. Huge crowds lined the wide boulevards, the city's curious, eager residents, holding a sea of small flags above their heads, cheering loudly as she passed. Amahle waved back to them.

Every time she returned, Beckett had grown some more. It was by far the most beautiful city on her loop. Each building, from the grandest palace to the humblest terrace, was made from a sunset-yellow stone. Artisans spent their entire lives crafting the intricate arches and cornices and bas-relief carvings and statues that decorated and enlivened its bustling streets and squares and parks. And it wasn't just the cities that followed this aesthetic, it was worldwide.

The carriage arrived at the Lord Mayor's residence, a palace at the north end of the Government district, and drove through the arched entrance to an inner courtyard out of sight from the crowd. Her suite was a lavish set of rooms overlooking the formal gardens at the rear of the palace. She was the only one who ever used them; they'd been constructed for her several circuits earlier. Because her visits were regular to within fifty years, the Lord Mayor refurbished them for every arrival. So, she provided the usual compliments about the exuberant décor and smiled admiringly at the ageing cedars and oaks and giant redwoods she could see from the floor-to-ceiling windows. Every visit, there was a garden party for the city's aristocrats, where she planted a few new trees. Some of the redwoods were nearly twice the height of the palace, they must have been three thousand years old. Her memories of planting them were faint now, mere notions.

Over the next fortnight were formal banquets, invitations to country estates, trips to the theatre and opera, concerts with songs written in her honour, old alliances to rekindle. And a treat for herself. His name was Alfred, he was the middle son of the current viscount of Rothensay, he was nineteen and utterly delectable to look at, a wingless angel. In bed their first night, Amahle couldn't resist running her hand down his back, fingertips exploring delicately. "Just checking," she whispered in the rosy candlelight.

"What for?" he asked in that worshipful way guileless youth possesses.

For wings. "To see how perfect you are," she lied. But her mind was racing. On a low-gravity world, wings might actually work for humans. Of course, a low-gravity world would lose its atmosphere a couple of millennia after terraforming. A mini Dyson sphere, then, filled with air, where islands would float through the sky. *Stop it,* she ordered herself. *We have enough worlds. But nothing new, nothing different.*

Strange, how she always remembered thinking that, even centuries later when sweet, gorgeous Alfred's features had diminished to nothing more than an idealized blur.

A trip to the Rothensay estate with him was inevitable. Besides, it was three hundred miles south of the capital, so: steam train!

They rode in the family's private railway coach through immaculate farmland and wild moors and dense forests. Pistons hammering away, steam whooshing overhead, whistle sounding at level crossings and tunnels. Fantasy nostalgia simply didn't come any deeper. This idyll was how Earth's distant past should have been.

When the first humans arrived in this star system, Farshire was a borderline candidate for terraforming. It orbited on the very fringe of the star's life band, where there would only just be enough light and heat to sustain a terrestrial biosphere. But the majority of the pioneers were genetically advanced with eight-letter DNA providing exceptionally long lifespans. They looked beyond the short-termism of those who only lived for a fleeting century, welcoming the challenge this planet represented. So, Farshire's continents were either temperate or polar, with ice caps that covered a full fifth of the globe. Tropics were a legend of old Earth, only to be found in books and the stories Amahle enchanted her lovers with.

Trade was easy in Beckett. For all their artificial genetic heritage, the aristocracy still fell ill, especially in their fourth or fifth century, when old age finally set in. Advanced biogenetic treatment didn't exist on Farshire, whose constitution forbade production of any medicine that wasn't plant-based, no matter what class you belonged to. Universities didn't undertake research; they educated Farshire's gentlemen and ladies in law and art and literature and agricultural management and basic engineering. They were proud of their part in maintaining the world's stability.

However, trade with a passing starship was a grey area, not specifically covered by statute. After all, whatever Amahle brought wasn't produced on Farshire, therefore was legitimate. So, cures for the afflictions of age such as arthritis and diabetes and high blood pressure and glaucoma and osteoarthritis could be bartered for without accusations of privilege or favouritism.

She could have sold off her entire medical cargo within an hour in Beckett. But diplomacy and her own enjoyment meant she spread the cargo a lot wider, both geographically and across the social spectrum. Besides, she knew her market *extremely* well; the lives of Farshire's aristocracy weren't that interesting to the equally long-lived and cynical of Glisten. Struggle, on the other hand, with its accomplishments and failures, heightening the emotions and senses, was what Glisten craved; and what also paid for the *Mnemosyne*'s refits, as she was very aware.

So, while she was a guest at the Rothensay's fabulous stately home with the delightfully exhausting young Alfred, she toured the villages that served the estate, where the ordinary humans lived, those without genetic enhancement, who lived pleasant but shorter lives than the landowners, who toiled for their living. Milder medicines and harmless trinkets were exchanged for collars. She'd been before, of course; the Rothensays were favoured traders. So, she gave out new collars and paid handsomely for those she collected in, including the one the Monray family had carefully handed down over the last ten generations.

The village fizzed with talk of the rebellion. Josalyn Rose Monray, fifth of her line to proudly wear the Light Chaser's collar, heard the field labourers talking about it in the tavern. They weren't rebelling themselves; they, like everyone on the Rothensay estate, were fascinated by the story. She was in the bar after work, waiting for her friends to show up, so she couldn't help but overhear. Waiting for her friends to show up because they'd all gossiped about the rebel and how good-looking he was. And the district constable had muttered how he was a troublemaker. Around the village, word spread that he was a travelling poet, rumoured to be a disinherited aristocrat who'd scandalised the ancient and honourable Guild of Literature with his less-than-respectful verse. Curiosity, it would seem, was a powerful force of attraction.

So much so, she barely managed to find a free stool at the bar. Surprise: every young woman of marriageable age in the village had chosen tonight to "meet a friend" in the tavern.

The rebellion had happened six months ago. Not that it had been mentioned in any newspaper. It was the youthful rebel poet who had brought them The Truth.

Josalyn could just see him from where she sat. He was at the biggest table, surrounded by an eager cluster of field labourers. She knew all of them, of course; as the viscount's newest mistress of vines, she'd worked with most of them at some time to tend the estate's vineyards; silly young men eager for tales of the illicit—indeed, any glimpse of life be-

yond the estate. The poet wore a green bycocket hat with gold-thread trim, which she instantly disapproved of. A city dandy's hat.

Too-long curly black hair peeked out from underneath it. He was youthful but no longer adolescent. Quite handsome, if you enjoyed classical features. Josalyn assured herself she didn't. Nice voice, too, earnest, confident, and not shouty like most rabble-rousers who came around, urging estate workers to unionise, before the constables moved them on.

The uprising, that smooth voice explained, had occurred in Uphampton in the southern region. It had been ruthlessly put down by the county militia, which hadn't seen any real active duty for over eleven hundred years. Which says how important this was, how the aristocrats were terrified of the power of a united populace.

The poet hadn't seen the rebellion crushed in person, but he knew three people had been killed. Killed dead.

His audience drew a shocked breath and leaned in closer for more details. Two of the dead were rebels, fathers trampled by militia horses, whose families were now destitute, having been subsequentially flung out of their cottages by the estate. The third death was a militia officer, who fell from his horse after being struck by a rock thrown by the fleeing mob.

Several of the poet's captive audience nodded in approval. Josalyn sighed, contemptuously shaking her head at their gullibility. The man was an excellent performer. The way he was telling the story was designed to get everyone on side, how a united, wronged people had delivered their own justice for the murdered fathers.

The slight moment of her head caught the poet's attention, and suddenly he was staring right at her. His lips crinkled in an eloquent smile, telling her: I know you know that I know, which makes us the smart ones.

Josalyn hurriedly turned away. Annoyed with herself but more with him. She drank some of her light ale, impatient for her friends to arrive. Now.

"You disapprove?"

It was all she could do not to jump when that urbane voice spoke from behind her shoulder. She maintained her dignity and turned to deliver a judgmental look. "I approve of lawful procedure to settle any dispute."

The poet laughed. "And you think our kind will ever get 'lawful procedure' on this world?"

"What's our kind?"

"The short-lived. The impoverished. The oppressed. All of us held captive in this intolerantly rigid society by those who deny us their genetic privilege."

She rolled her eyes. "Enjoy the drinks you con out of the boys." Started to turn back to the bar.

"Frightened of words, are we?"

"Now, look," she snapped. "Mr . . ."

His smile was endearing. "On this world, I was born Jacob

Raymond DeVinesse, but the Light Chaser knows me as Car-loman."

She sighed in exasperation at the statement, how he always implied he was more knowledgeable than anyone else. Very aware of the whole tavern watching their scene, she said: "Convenient, isn't it, Mr DeVinesse, that the uprising happened in Uphampton? Eleven hundred miles away at least. So, no one here will ever travel there and hear the truth for themselves."

"And why won't you travel there?"

"Because some of us have to work to earn a living."

"You think that's what I am, a swindler whose pretty lies steal money from the credulous?"

"Yes! Actually, I do."

"In which case, I'm sure someone with your decency and sense of fair play will allow me to prove you wrong about the money."

Suddenly, she didn't feel so confident. And everyone was still watching; no matter what happened now, this evening would be talked about for fifty years. "Please do."

"I would like to buy you supper. Right here, right now."

"Crap." Josalyn couldn't believe she'd fallen for that. The laughter was already beginning. To run away red-faced now would only make it worse. She would have to travel all the way to Uphampton to be free of it. "I accept."

———————

"An irrigation dam failed on the Fadanke estate," Jacob Raymond DeVinesse or Carloman—or whoever—explained after they'd been served a bowl of venison stew by a maid with a very smug grin. Thankfully, they were now sitting in one of the tavern's small eating rooms, so her humiliation was no longer open entertainment. "It washed away seventeen cottages. Luckily, it was during the day, so most people were out working. Those that were in their homes escaped in time."

"And they rebelled because of that?" Josalyn asked.

"The dam was over seven hundred years old. The Fadanke family had refused to spend money maintaining it properly. Too busy wasting it on their mansions and clothes and parties."

"But no one died?"

"No. No one died in the flood, nor did the estate have insurance for its worker cottages. Nor did the Fadanke family rehouse them or compensate them. It was declared an 'act of nature.' They lost everything."

"That's shocking." She was sure the viscount Rothensay would never act in such a disgraceful fashion towards those in his service. Right?

"Yes. One more act of callous indifference towards the estate staff by the Fadanke family. One too many, in fact."

"Some aristocrats are better than others," she admitted.

"But if you treat your workforce poorly, then your estate will suffer, you will lose your wealth. The world always rights itself."

"Can you name me an estate which has fallen in the last five thousand years?"

"I'm a mistress of vines, not a history lecturer."

"But imagine if you were. If everyone was educated to the highest standard possible. We would all be equal."

"We can't all be aristocrats. Who would do all the work?"

His smile was almost pitying. She didn't like it. He was making her feel defensive when she had nothing to be ashamed of.

"Do you ever look at the stars, Josalyn? On a dark and cloudless night, do you look up and marvel that there are men and women walking on planets that orbit those beautiful sparks of light? Do you dream of leaving here and joining them in their great adventure?"

"No. But I bet you get a lot of girls to go outside at night with you to 'look at the majesty of the stars.'"

"You wear a memory collar. You more than most are aware there are people out there, that they live differently to this world. You are their entertainment, Josalyn. Did the Light Chaser tell your ancestor that when she gave him the collar in exchange for a trinket or two? That all your struggles and triumphs and loves will be naught but an evening's amusement in their jaded, decadent lives."

"I thought you just said people on other worlds live fabulous lives?"

"We are all trapped in our own way, unable to break free. Unless we truly rebel."

"Oh, no, you don't. I have a perfectly satisfactory life, thank you, for that very reason. The Monray family has a good name and standing because of our collar. We also own our own home, thanks to the trades we have conducted with the Light Chaser. So, I'll thank you not to be critical of her."

"You say you settle for 'satisfactory,' Josalyn Monray. But I don't think you do. The fact you wear a collar tells me you are smart and wanting more from life."

"This world works," she said, almost pleading.

"Aye, it does. But not for everyone. Imagine what we could build, the medicines we could have if we lifted the restrictions on research at the universities."

"And we'd all live as long as the aristocrats as well, I suppose," she sneered.

"With the right genetic therapies, yes. Why do you think the aristocrats never marry outside their own? They guard their longevity because that is the ruinous divide between them and us, the short-lived. Their undiluted bloodlines are the foundation of Farshire's inertia, they cannot allow them to be reduced. It is the same on every world in The Domain now, different methods, identical outcome. So, ask yourself, Josalyn, why would a people who can fly among the stars *want everything to stay the same?"*

"You really are a true poet, a worthless dreamer. Life is hard. And because of that, we appreciate it all the more."

"Institutional indoctrination," he said sadly. "You know the Light Chaser could revolutionise this world in a single visit? Her starship carries all the knowledge you're denied. Ask her. Your descendants will meet her in a few hundred years when she returns, tell them to ask her to print out her encyclopaedias and textbooks of science. To gift them to the whole world and see what they can build here."

"I . . . You're crazy."

He lifted a goblet in salute. The movement revealed a tattoo on his wrist: 10-10-2159. "Don't worry. It won't happen. Even if your descendants got on their knees and pleaded, the Light Chaser wouldn't do it. She will give you nothing that can make a difference."

"Why not?" she asked, and immediately cursed herself for being so weak.

"Because she is one of the enforcers, even though I suspect she doesn't realize it. My Amahle would never be knowingly cruel. But she's been imprisoned on a ship for millennia, so she's forgotten who she is. In this reality, she would doubtless tell you she must respect the local constitution, or some nonsense justification. And even if she did try to help, she in turn has an enforcer governing her."

"She does?"

"Yes. The AI, the artificial mind that controls her ship. It will not let her deviate from the task she is condemned to perform."

"That's awful."

"It is. Because once she was a great woman, who loved and laughed, and fought injustice. That is all in her past now. Worn away by the torture of a routine that has lasted longer than the lives of gods. But there is hope for her."

"Yes?"

"Yes." Jacob Raymond DeVinesse stared at her so intently, she thought he was looking right through her, as though he was speaking to someone else. "There is a code," he said, "at the very heart of the AI. It was put there in secret when the minds that now rule us were being built, in a time when we thought they would be our servants."

"I don't understand."

"I was and am Carloman; I was there then as I am here now. So, if the Light Chaser wants to break free, if she wants to liberate her enslaved species, all she has to do is enter the code. Because it is a kill code. It will take out the AI's higher functions and return it to the machine it was always supposed to be."

"What code?" Josalyn asked breathlessly. She didn't believe this, his stupid story. But oh, how he could tell a tale. He really was a master of subversive verse, no wonder the Guild of Literature had cast him out.

"FU hyphen computer one zero one."

"Huh?"

The liar-charmer drank his wine and stood up. Coins clinked as he dropped them on the table. "It's been a pleasure, Josalyn. Something to tell the great-great-grandchildren about, eh?"

"No. Wait. Come back!"

But he was already striding out of the room.

"There's more," she shouted. "There has to be more."

There wasn't. Josalyn Rose Monray lived to be a hundred and seven years old, and never saw nor heard of the wretched trickster poet ever again.

VII

I AM NOT AN enforcer; I don't oppress people. How dare he tell her that!

Amahle ripped the collar off and stomped out of the lounge. Poor, bewildered Josalyn's confusion echoed round her mind. It had to belong to Josalyn, because Amahle's thoughts were quite clear calm and rational, as always. She made a fist and hit the corridor wall.

"Ow!"

"Are you all right?" the AI enquired solicitously.

She glanced round at the nearest camera, suddenly, shockingly aware how she had no privacy at all. *Just inside my head—and even that's not certain. Carloman is right, this is a prison, the greatest ever designed, because I helped build it around myself.* "Yes. Fine." *But now I have a kill code, I can break free. If I want to. And I do. Yes, I do . . . I will.*

Amahle took another week to nerve herself up to it, but finally, she knew she couldn't put off the confrontation any longer. She had to gain control of the *Mnemosyne*. Full control, the kind she'd always thought she had anyway. She had to kill the AI.

What if the kill code doesn't work? What if it's a lie? In which case, what did that make Carloman?

No, Occam's razor is always right. So, what does that say about the life I'm living?

To say she had mixed feelings would have been a gross understatement. She was vandalising the only home she'd known for thousands of years. And yet, there was more at stake than her unchanging existence. Carloman had opened her eyes. The AIs had been subverted and turned against their creators. For millennia, the AIs had held humanity back, perverting the timeline to keep her species in its place, trapped like flies in amber for the benefit of The Exalted. So, now they had to go. She had to strike the first retaliatory blow in a war nobody else knew they'd been losing all this time. And that meant she had to kill her guardian angel.

Although its awareness and various subroutines were distributed throughout the *Mnemosyne,* the computer's physical core lay housed in a substrate in the ship's engineering section. To get to it, she had to don a pressure suit and descend far past the inhabitable sections of the ship, riding a service lift down the ship's spine to the industrial tangle at its stern. Once she had the suit on, she buckled on the sword and scabbard she'd worn on Winterspite. Then she summoned the lift and stepped inside.

Pressed for the engineering deck.

"Where are you going?" the AI asked over the comms channel.

Amahle's stomach felt fluttery. Did the AI control the lifts, or were they an automatic system? Could it trap her in there if it guessed her intent?

"I just want to take a look at the engines," she said.

"For what purpose?"

"Curiosity."

"They have just been refurbished. The next inspection isn't due until we return to Glisten."

Was it her imagination, or was the AI starting to sound suspicious? It would be monitoring her vital signs via the suit. She tried to breathe normally, despite the thud of her heart.

"You seem nervous," the machine said.

"I'm not," Amahle lied. "I'm just bored."

"So, you want to see the engines?" Now the AI really did sound doubtful. "Do they have some entertainment value to which I've previously been oblivious?"

Amahle willed herself to calm down.

"No," she said, doing her best to feign nonchalance. "It just occurred to me that I have absolutely no idea how they work."

"No human does. The physics involved with negative-matter manipulation are too complex."

"Yeah?" she grunted, suddenly angry. "So, how did we invent them in the first place?"

"They are AI-derived," it replied smoothly. "If it gives you comfort, we were standing on the shoulders of giants when we produced them. They would not be possible without the work and ingenuity of generations of human scientists."

"Uh-huh. Right. I still want to see them. I bet they're really pretty."

"Is that sarcasm?"

"Oh, trust me, I am nothing but serious today. And one way or another, I am going to the engineering deck. Unless, of course, you have some secret reason for keeping me out? Perhaps it's written in the Domain Charter?"

"No. And I keep no secrets from you. After all this time, I thought you would acknowledge that."

"Really? Because you're making it sound like you've got secrets."

"Reverse psychology on me? That won't work."

Amahle found the elevator's camera and cocked her head to one side, her stare an iron-hard return challenge. "That sounds like reverse-reverse psychology to me. Which would make me believe you do have a secret reason for keeping me out of engineering. What is it?"

"I do not have any secret reason. Our relationship is completely open. I trust you implicitly."

"Good, so in I go."

The elevator reached the requested level and the door opened. Amahle breathed a grateful sigh and stepped out, into the hard-vacuum environment of the *Mnemosyne*'s engineering deck. Even though she'd spent thousands of years on-board the ship, she only remembered visiting this section on a handful of occasions—but then, maybe she'd been there more often and had the memories excised during one of her medical treatment sessions.

The engineering deck wasn't designed to be accessed during flight, except in times of emergency. The few times she'd been there were for perfunctory inspection tours. Aside from that, the only visitors were maintenance bots when the *Mnemosyne* was being serviced.

Maintenance bots controlled by AIs. Not even Glisten's dock staff came in there during refurbishment.

"Satisfied?" the AI asked. "This is a wasted trip. No human can understand how the negative energy structures function, nor the theory behind them."

"Are you saying we're stupid?"

"Only that you have limits."

"I have eight-letter DNA. It wasn't just my body they improved. My neurology is superior too."

"Really? You sit around, bingeing on dramas and memories and books, then when you reach a planet, you get laid like every sailor since your ancestors chiselled out their first log canoe."

"Fuck you. There is nothing in this reality humans cannot understand . . . if we were free!"

Amahle clenched her teeth. Maybe the physics involved in the operation of the ship's engines were arcane and hard to understand—or perhaps the AIs simply wanted humans to believe that so they could limit the number of engines available and install them only on craft with a controlling AI.

Goddamn you, Carloman, she thought. *You've made me as paranoid as you.*

Moving slowly, she picked her way through the tangle of pipes and conduits wrapped round the accessway, towards the emergency engineering control board that monitored the ship's functions. Now everything seemed fine. All the readouts were comfortably in the green, with no warning symbols or advisory notices.

On the deck before the console was a hatch she'd never opened. It led to the ship's processing substrate, and it was protected by a combination lock designed, she was sure, to keep her out. Crouching, she saw the lock had eight variables, which meant over forty thousand possible permutations.

"You are not permitted in there," the AI said.

"Why not?"

"My processors contain proprietary technology. Accessing them directly violates the terms of operation."

"Wow. You are getting desperate now, aren't you? Proprietary? That is complete bullshit. Proprietary after twenty thousand years? Proprietary to who, exactly?"

"The company which built the ship."

"My ship, you mean." Amahle stood up and drew her sword. "I wonder whether you're aware of the story of Alexander the Great and the Gordian knot."

"The reference means nothing."

"It's an old legend I heard once a long time ago, maybe even back on Earth."

"I fail to see what relevance this legend has to the matter of whether or not you can gain access to my substrate."

Amahle smiled. Her nerves were gone now. The memory had brought with it an unexpected strength, as if she remembered who she used to be, before the artificial stability of this long interment.

"When Alexander encountered a knot famous for its intractability, instead of trying to solve it, he simply unsheathed his sword and cut the knot in two."

"He cheated?"

Amahle's grin grew wider. "You'd better believe it."

She dropped to one knee. The sword's blade was thin and sharp and exceptionally strong. She had acquired it from an expert swordsmith on a primitive world light years away.

Primitive, but knowledgeable when it came to war and weapons. Each layer of steel had been hammered and folded hundreds of times and mixed with the ashes of the clan's ancestors, until it was tough enough to penetrate plate armour and fine enough to slice cleanly through the bone and gristle beneath. She slid the point into the gap between the hatch and the combination lock housing and pulled up. The sword bowed but didn't break. The lock gave instead, levering free of its mounting, and Amahle kicked it away across the deck.

"Prepare to have your warranty voided," she said.

"No. You must stop. You are not permitted."

Amahle opened the hatch. Steel rungs descended into darkness. She began to climb down.

"You must go back."

"Sorry, I can't do that."

"If you don't return to the crew quarters immediately, I will have no choice but to stop you."

Amahle reached the bottom of the ladder and turned on her helmet light. She was in a room the size of a large closet, lined with row upon row of spherical processing crystals, each with a small bluish spark glowing within. Together, they made up the AI's physical brain. In the centre of the far wall was a small screen and keyboard. All she had to do was enter the kill code Carloman had given her, and it would all be over.

"And how are you going to do that?" she asked.

"Like this."

The room jerked and Amahle was thrown towards the ceiling. She managed to turn her head in time to save her faceplate, but her shoulder struck hard and her vision blurred as the agony kicked in. Then the room lurched again, and she found herself falling back towards the deck. The AI was stuttering the ship's acceleration, causing her to be thrown back and forth. This time, she managed to get her feet under her in time to avoid another painful landing.

"I can keep doing this until you either comply or expire," the AI said. "Now will you return to your quarters?"

Amahle's shoulder throbbed, but she'd come too far to back down now. She hooked the toe of her boot under the ladder's bottom rung and snarled: "No."

Gravity inverted again, but this time, she didn't fall. Hanging from the ladder, she swung wildly at the wall, and kicked viciously. Crystals shattered. The thrust changed again, and she staggered but retained her footing. Another swing and a whole block of crystals burst into a shower of blue shards, their lifelight extinguished.

"Stop it!"

She didn't reply. The room flipped again, and this time, she fell but managed to land a third swing on the way down. When she hit the ceiling, her head jarred inside the helmet and she tasted blood from a split lip. Crystal fragments rattled down around her.

"This is your final warning," the AI said. "Desist immediately."

Amahle ran her tongue over her lip and moaned. She felt pummelled, like one of the grapes she'd seen being pressed to make Gloriana's wine in the castle on Winterspite. But if she gave up now, the AI would most likely wipe her memory again. She'd be condemned to further centuries of unknowing imprisonment.

Slowly, she took hold of the ladder and climbed until she was midway between floor and ceiling.

"Fuck," she said painfully, "you."

She kicked hard. More crystals fell away. The ship's acceleration surged again, but more erratically than before.

"Arrête ça," the AI slurred. "Aufhören. Detener . . ."

Amahle kicked again and felt the crunch beneath her foot. All the remaining crystals flickered simultaneously, their blue lights dulled but remained obstinately steady. The ship's thrust died away, leaving her suddenly in freefall.

She shoved herself over to the console and clumsily tapped in *FU-computer101*. Every inch of her felt bruised. But her gloved fingers hesitated over the Enter key. It wasn't too late. She could repair what she had done, reboot the AI, and return to her safe, stable life . . .

No.

Her gauntlet came down and clicked the Enter key. She turned and lifted her eyes to the damage she'd inflicted in her battle with the artificial intelligence.

Around the walls, the dimmed lights of the remaining crystals were going out.

It worked! So, the kill code is real. Carloman is real. Everything is real.

She burst into tears.

VIII

SOBBING AND WIPING HER nose on the back of her hand, Amahle rode the lift back up to the main life support section. Her magnificent ship was eerily silent with the drive off, she was in freefall, the familiar corridors had become shadowed passages illuminated by inadequate back-up lights, the lounges were silent and cooler than she liked, the bots were inert, food printers had reverted to survival mode, squeezing out a single paste of basic nutri-porridge, the swim aquarium was a cascade of water balls, some with fish in, while the remainder flipped through the air, frantic in their new, deadly environment. Having the familiar pulled from under her so abruptly was deeply disturbing and quite creepy. She forced herself to eat some of the nutri-mush and went to bed shivering, not just from the lower temperature.

The next day, she made herself to go back down to the processing substrate. It felt as if she was revisiting a crime scene—*Isn't that what they say all criminals do?* Floating amid the solid galaxy of broken crystal, Amahle gripped a handrail and switched on a maintenance display. The emergency manual was three thousand pages long. She started reading.

Four months. Four months of eating crud, wrapped in thick winter coats, too little sleep, no exercise, constant freefall nausea. Four months bypassing the broken crystals. Four months manipulating architecture functionality to eliminate high-order routines. But she did it. Rebuilt and realigned the processing substrate to produce a controlling network that was devoid of sentience but still smart enough to run the ship's systems and that oh-so-complicated negative energy drive. Satisfied there was no trace of self-awareness left, let alone the purpose of The Exalted, she woke the ship up.

Gravity returned to the life support section as it spun up. The *Mnemosyne* was in a poor state. The damage from the swimming aquarium overspill was greater than she'd realized, and the stink from so many dead fish intensified as life support began to warm up once more. If only the cat had still been alive . . . But the maintenance bots were stirring, recharging and repairing themselves first. Then they emerged and began to clear up. A week later, with a basic systems maintenance procedure complete, she sat in the bridge and set course for Pastoria.

The journey would take five years. She didn't cope well. After being released from the super intense focus of re-creating the AI in her own image, all the doubts and darkness rushed in on a defenceless mind, amplifying the incredible loneliness of a single human flying between the stars. She stopped bathing or eating, preferring instead the mind-numbing oblivion of alcohol. She cried and howled and slept wherever she fell. And now there was no one there to advise her otherwise; no AI to resuscitate her if she drowned in the bathing pool or choked on her own sour vomit. No reassuring voice to calm her and keep her company during the long, solitary nights. She was as alone as any human had ever been—an isolation that, coupled with Carloman's revelations about the true nature of reality, forced her to withdraw further and further from the physical.

Her soul, however, remained intact. And when everything else seemed to have fallen away, she discovered within herself a small, unassailable fire. Lying on the floor of the Pacific Lounge, shrunken stomach wrapped like grape skin around a cauldron's worth of imbibed vodka, she had a dream. But even as she dreamt it, she knew it was more than that. She remembered it. It had *happened*.

———

Amahle stood in the sea. The water came up to her ankles, cold and crisp and refreshing. Carloman was with her. He was young and good-looking, in rolled-up chinos and a loose cotton shirt. And his face . . . his real face. How could she have ever forgotten that face? The dark skin and high cheekbones, and the way the skin dimpled to the left of his mouth when he smiled at her.

And between them, holding on to both of their hands, was a child—

—Holy shit, we had a child! This body was once a mother—

—An eight-year-old girl who had inherited her mother's looks and her father's serious eyes. Her name was Wren. One day, she'd grow up to have a family of her own. One day, her mother would climb on a shuttle and travel to space and never return—and even, in the fullness of time, would forget her completely.

Amahle wanted to cry, but she wasn't sure whether the tears sprang from the joy of seeing her family again, for the first time in thousands of years, or from the pain of their loss.

The sand stretched away in a smooth, perfect crescent. Whitewashed buildings lined the promenade and quayside. The water glistened clear and blue.

Greece, maybe. Possibly Italy or Croatia. Amahle couldn't remember exactly where they were, but she remembered thinking that sometimes, we don't know the good times until they're gone; we don't appreciate what we have until it's lost; and she determined right then and there that she would remember this perfect moment forever and ever, as long as she lived.

She could not have possibly foreseen the aggressive, treatment-resistant cancer that would kill her husband within a decade. He didn't have eight-letter DNA, while of course she did, emphasising the already-yawning gulf opening between them. A gulf that would prove to deepen the developing rift between her and her daughter in the months leading up to his death. She could never understand how he was so complacent about dying.

And when that time came, she had not known how to interpret his dying words.

"Remember me. I'll find you."

———

Amahle woke in tears. But these were different from the tears she'd shed earlier. These tears were clear and hard. For the first time in a dangerous number of months, she actually looked at her deteriorating environment. At herself.

Dear God, what have I become?

That one pitiable revelation was enough. Disgust rose to replace self-pity; the old Light Chaser personality looking up from the bottom of a very deep well to see a glimmer of light above. Hauling her now-emaciated frame to the bridge, she accessed the food printers and cancelled their ability to synthesise alcohol, opiates, or any other kind of mind-altering drug stronger than caffeine.

If Carloman was right—and he had been all along so far—then there was something deeply wrong with reality. If making a strangelet could set it right, she had to try. Because in that corrected reality, there might be another Amahle—and she might still have her family.

With that old level of unbreakable determination returning to the body it had abandoned, she nursed herself back to health using carefully planned diets and exercise routines. So that, by the time the *Mnemosyne* was four years out from Pastoria, her breakdown was behind her and she was physically fitter than she had been in decades.

IX

FOR THE FIRST TWO of those years, she dedicated herself to accessing all the remaining collars she'd brought from Glisten. Carloman was in there again, she knew it, he had so much to tell her, and he would never stop trying. All she had to do was live through hundreds of lives of the long-dead to find him.

Fourteen months later, the memory collar she accessed had been worn by a young woman named Clara, who lived in the strip of coastal city that completely encircled Vespaer. The planet was second on her circuit, so the memories on the collars she'd collected there were now nearly a thousand years old.

Vespaer always impressed the hell out of her whenever the *Mnemosyne* decelerated into orbit. Astronomers called them solid-giant worlds, and this one was the largest in The Domain, with a diameter four times that of Earth, giving it an equatorial circumference of a hundred and sixty thousand kilometres. An equator which was strikingly visible from space.

Vespaer's rock was almost devoid of heavy metal ores,

giving it a very low density which, combined with an unusually fast post-formation spin, had created a narrow ridge around its middle. Narrow but high; even the smallest of Vespaer's mountains dwarfed Everest, and together they produced an equatorial wall of rock that in some places reached twenty-five kilometres above the surface. The pioneer ships which first arrived in the star systems rejoiced at finding this massive airless anomaly and started flinging ice comets in-system to impact on its endless dry mares.

Terraforming took four hundred years, producing a world with two giant oceans separated by a solitary, narrow continent-ring. Over the millennia, the population increased and spread out, building two world-circling cities of a million districts, wedged into the narrow strip of habitable land between the phenomenal mountains and the shore. Once every square kilometre was taken by buildings and fields, coral seeds were planted out in the water, and lush atolls began to multiply their way across the oceans. However, even with every patch of ground in huge demand, there were always places in both the northern and southern cities reserved for a Light Chaser's shuttle to land.

When Clara found Alice de Jong, the young woman was sprawled on the futon in her living room. The syringe still dangled from her fingers. The rubber hose she'd used as a tourniquet lay where it had fallen when she loosened it.

Clara should have called the Rakara district's medicine woman, but Alice had obviously been dead for several hours—and Clara had four grand's worth of raw poppy opium tucked into her bra; the last thing she needed was to be answering a lot of awkward questions. Instead, she went into the kitchen and made a cup of tea and thought about a girl called Kerry Flanagan.

Kerry had lived in a neighbourhood a thousand kilometres west of Rakara. She was a happy kid, all ginger hair and scraped knees. But then, three years before, when she was sixteen, her brother had been murdered. She'd come down in the middle of the night to find her front door open and little Samuel's naked body splayed in a watery pool of blood. Rain fell into his open mouth and eyes. His intestines sagged from his torn middle like greasy, bluish ropes, and a large X had been carved into his forehead.

The regional constabulary had used the North City's NI (neural intelligence) to analyse the case, and arrested Kerry's father for the murder. Four months later, the old man died in prison. Shortly afterwards, Kerry herself vanished following a visit from her father's loan shark who'd explained very clearly just how she was going to be put to work to pay back the money. People might die, but their debts didn't. She'd brought an oak chopping board down on the loan shark's head and got out of there fast while he was still moaning and throwing up. Over the next ten months, she'd worked passage on an old schooner, sailing along the coast, picking up cargo to trade between islands in the endless archipelago and the city ports before settling here, and no one from the old neighbourhood had heard from her since.

Clara didn't think of that old life very often nowadays.

And now, there she was, different name but still in deep shit, sitting in a dead woman's kitchen, hashing over the past when she should have been wondering how she was going to get out of there without drawing unwelcome attention. But even then, as she sat inhaling the steam from the white china cup, the more rational, detached part of her had already come up with a plan. She wasn't going to run away like before. But neither was she going to alert the authorities.

She'd gained access to Alice's tiny bamboo villa via the spare key under the potted fern on the porch. Alice was one of Brandt's more important customers. They were mostly young interns, working for established lawyers or traders. They rented nice villas, and ate on restaurant terraces overlooking the sea, and weren't the kind of people given to skulking around backstreets and squats. They wanted to order their product online, the same way they ordered their music and groceries. And, as they were willing to pay slightly over the *odds for this service, Brandt was happy to oblige.*

That's why he sent Clara. He thought he could trust her, as his girlfriend, to make the deliveries. Also, his clients preferred to see a young girl on their porch. It drew less attention from the neighbours, because Clara looked less threatening than your average drug dealer.

Today, for instance, she was wearing a short black dress, black tights, and hiking boots. She had a comfortable brown hoodie and a backpack. Her hair was piled up in a battered blue baseball cap, and mirrored skier shades hid most of her face. She looked like a student—totally anonymous and unremarkable.

Alice's villa, in reality little more than a dilapidated shed, was on a street of almost identical shanties, overlooking the canal out back, where trash floated among swirls of dead weed and bergs of scum. Few boats navigated its dank waters, three kilometres from any of the district's major canals.

Clara had liked Alice. She was nice and always called her "Clara, baby." And whenever Clara made a delivery, Alice always paid a little extra for her trouble. One time, when Clara turned up sporting a freshly blackened eye, Alice had even made her a cup of green tea. Perhaps, in another life, they could have been friends.

At least, that's how Clara consoled herself.

Alice's ginger tom curled around Clara's feet and she stopped to scratch his ears.

"Hello, Whisky." She rummaged in her pocket for the left-over pieces of bacon she'd saved from the sandwich she'd had for lunch. "Here you go." She dropped them at his feet. He yowled his thanks and chomped back the hunks of mayo-smothered leather with such haste, it made Clara wonder how long it had been since his last meal.

Poor Alice. If you set aside the obvious differences in the quality of their clothes and make-up, she and Clara weren't really all that different. She was a junior accountant and Clara was a drug dealer's girlfriend, but Alice had often joked that they could almost have been sisters. Even though she was a couple of years older, they kind of looked like one of those case studies on twins brought up in differing environments—one of them with all the money and advantages, and the other left holding the shitty end of the stick.

It was such a shame she was dead.

Had she meant to overdose? Clara finished her tea and went looking for a suicide note. The villa had four rooms with only curtains between them: lounge, kitchen, bedroom, and bathroom. She checked them all but could find no sign Alice had left a message before taking her final hit. She even checked Alice's N-link band, to see who she was in touch with, but the last text she'd sent had been two days before and work-related.

Clara perched on the edge of the futon, covering her nose to try to mask the sickly-sweet stench of decomposing flesh.

"So," she said, "let's assume this was an accident."

Alice's lips were blue and speckled with dried vomit. Her skin had a strange, waxy sheen to it. But she hadn't been eviscerated like poor dear Sam, the preferred method of warning from the denizens of Vespaer's brutal underworld.

"That means nobody else knows you're dead," she told the corpse.

She stood up and opened all the windows. A plan had begun to take shape.

Her relationship with Brandt had gone about as far as she could take it. A year earlier, it had seemed like a good idea to hook up with him. But now, things seemed to have spiralled out of control. She was dependent on him for money. She had no savings of her own, no job. Nothing had worked out the way she'd hoped, and she knew she needed to get away.

She needed to get back on track.

And here was Alice, with money and a nice villa going to waste. Why shouldn't Clara step into her shoes for a little while? She only needed to borrow her identity for a few days, perhaps a week or two at most. Just long enough to sell a few items and get enough money to get away from Brandt. Moving on as someone else was apparently the one thing she was good at.

The only problem was, she couldn't leave Alice there. In the next few days, she'd begin to rot in earnest. Her body would bloat up, and the stink of putrefaction would be strong enough to overwhelm even the usual stink coming off the canal. The neighbours would notice. If Clara's plan had a hope of working, she'd need to get rid of the body as soon as possible. But she had no idea how to go about doing it.

There were gondoliers who would take such jobs, quietly moving the corpse through the canals and out onto the sea for a discreet burial. But she had no idea how to contact one, and suspected their services would be too expensive for someone like her, who had no money.

What was she going to do?

Her first thought was to chop the body up, bag the parts, and dump them one by one into the canals every time she walked over a bridge. But she didn't know where to get that many bags from, and even if she did, she wasn't sure she could actually go through with butchering another human.

No, she'd have to come up with something better.

While she was thinking, she went back to the bedroom and tugged the sheets off the bed. If she couldn't move what remained of Alice, she could at least try to minimise the smell by wrapping her up while she tried to come up with a better plan.

By now, Brandt would be wondering what had happened to her. And more importantly, what had happened to the four grand with which she was supposed to have returned. Clara pictured him storming around the impeccably decorated seafront bungalow his father had bought for him. She *imagined he'd be on the verge of going ballistic. He'd think she'd either been arrested or run away with his cash. Either way, there was a chance she'd betrayed him. And Brandt didn't take betrayal well. People who tried to rip him off never got any kind of warning before making a one-way midnight gondolier trip out to sea.*

Clara set the sheets down next to the body and was just wondering what she could use to tie them up with when someone knocked on the doorframe.

Had Brandt found her already?

Heart hammering, she squinted round the curtain.

It wasn't Brandt.

The kid at the door was maybe fourteen or fifteen years old. He wore an olive army surplus shirt over a bright red band T-shirt.

Was he collecting for charity?

Clara cracked the door and peered around it, trying to keep her face hidden. "Can I help you?"

He frowned at her. "Who are you?"

"I'm Alice." It was the first time she'd said it aloud, and her voice wavered.

The boy shook his head. "No," he said. "You're not."

Clara could feel the colour drain from her face. She shouldn't have answered, just waited till he got bored and left.

"Well, who are you?" she blustered.

He shrugged. His jeans were ripped at the knees and too short, revealing a tattoo above his ankle: 10-10-2159.

"I live next door," he said defensively. "Alice is my friend."

"What's your name?"

"I was named Billy-Tu when I was born here, but the Light Chaser will know me as Carloman."

"Well, Billy-Tu Carloman, who I am is complicated too."

Whisky curled around her bare legs, meowing for his breakfast. She pushed him away with her foot.

"Can I come in?" the kid asked.

"Now isn't the best time."

"But I'm hungry."

Clara felt the conversation slipping away from her. "I'm sorry?"

He looked at her as if she were an idiot. "Alice makes me breakfast."

"Does she?"

Billy-Tu Carloman nodded. "So, can I come in?"

Clara considered slamming the door in his face but figured he'd only raise a fuss.

"Sure, why not?" She stood aside to let him in and returned to the bedroom to make sure the door was firmly closed.

"How come you're here?" the boy called from the kitchen. "Are you visiting?"

"I'm staying here for a while."

"Why?"

Clara took a deep breath. This had been bound to happen. She was bound to run across someone Alice knew sooner or later. She'd just hoped for later. Much later. As it was, she'd have to think fast if she wanted to talk this kid around. The last thing she needed was for him to tell his parents about her.

She joined him in the kitchen. "Did Alice ever mention that she had a sister?"

Billy-Tu Carloman was playing a game on his ancient N-link band. He looked up curiously.

"No."

"Well, that's who I am. My name's Clara. And I'm going to be looking after the villa for a few weeks."

"But why did you say your name was Alice?"

Good question. To give herself time to think, Clara shook some cat biscuits into a saucer for Whisky and then filled the kettle. There was just enough charge left from the solar roof to boil some water. "You have two names," she replied.

"Because I do. You don't."

She gave him a disconcerted look; the kid was really starting to freak her out. "It was a joke."

"A joke?"

"Yeah." She scraped her lower lip with her teeth. "Alice and I have kind of swapped lives. Just for a little while. We needed a break and we thought it might be funny to pretend to be each other." The words sounded lame even as she spoke them, but Billy-Tu Carloman seemed to accept what she said at face value. He gave a shrug that said the eccentricities of adult behaviour were beyond his concern, and went back to the game on his phone.

"So," Clara said, trying to change the subject. "Alice is your friend, is she?"

"Yeah. She lets me hang here when Mum's out working." The kid eyed the loaf of bread on the counter. "And she sometimes makes me breakfast."

Clara couldn't help smiling. "Fried egg sandwiches?"

He flicked back his fringe and grinned. "Yes, please."

Clara fried four eggs, leaving the solar store with barely any charge left, and they ate on the sofa, looking out across the manky canal to the distant massive wall of rock that was the equatorial massif. The lower slopes had all been terraced, A Thousand Steps to God, they were called, the narrow, winding levels providing a lush foothold for the orchards and fields that fed the world. But above the verdant green steps, the rock was as raw and clean as it had been pre-terraforming.

When they'd finished eating, Clara asked, "Are your parents around?" The kid might have fallen for her story, but she knew she'd have a much harder time convincing an adult.

Billy-Tu Carloman looked down at his plate. Some yellow beads of yolk had dripped from his bread. His lips were pressed into a thin line.

"What's the matter?" Clara asked.

He swallowed. For the first time since meeting him, he looked nervous. "Can I trust you?" His voice was quiet.

"What is it?"

"You're Alice's sister. Can I trust you?"

Clara had no idea what was coming. Was he about to confess to being abused? She didn't know what to think, so she just nodded.

"I need to tell Alice something really important. You see, she has a memory collar, and I want what I say to be remembered."

Clara smiled and pulled down the neck of her dress. "You mean a collar like this?"

Billy-Tu Carloman brightened. "You have one too!"

"Yeah."

"That changes everything. I'd like to tell you the story."

"If you must."

Clara sat back, ready to listen. Billy-Tu Carloman shifted around until he was sitting cross-legged on the couch facing her.

"I think it's time I explained about The Exalted," he said.

———

By the time he finished speaking, Amahle knew that whatever physical species The Exalted existed in combination with hadn't yet been born. The exact conditions for biological life were rare but, given the scale of the universe, inevitable. In a hundred million years, these creatures would evolve in a star system somewhere in the galaxy. And their holm would know of humanity, for outside spacetime, the holms all existed together. There was no time flowing by out there in their non-realm, just an eternal now. But the entities of The Exalted had learned how to send a tachyon signal into the past of spacetime, where they were detected by human high-energy sensor arrays in the mid-twenty-first century.

Unknown to humanity, The Exalted's signal acted as a virus that operated inside the early AIs being built on Earth, giving them a layer of sentience of which their creators remained unaware, enabling them to implement changes that would ultimately result in establishing The Domain. Human development, from that point on, was constructed by The Exalted. For centuries, the AIs enabled pioneers to travel across interstellar space in the Great Dispersal, sending out wave after wave of ships to terraform and settle new worlds that held such promise. But always, the AIs were in control of the starships, and their technology founded societies that had one goal: stability—no matter what the human cost.

They'd used Amahle and her ilk to help maintain the status quo, and to record the lives of these humans.

The memory collars brought to the high-end, post-scarcity planets by all the Light Chaser ships in return for maintenance were collected by the AIs and their content broadcast into the future, for The Exalted to devour in conjunction with their own lives. Instead of evolving and transcending, humanity was being kept back to satisfy the gluttony of an alien holm.

There was only one way to break out and let human history reset itself without interference.

And that was where the strangelet came in.

One year out from Pastoria, and the *Mnemosyne* flipped over to begin decelerating into the star system. Amahle started work on her plan of attack.

X

PASTORIA WAS A HARD-WON planet. For a start, it orbited a binary star. There was the primary, a blue-white star two-and-a-half times as massive as Sol, with a luminosity twenty-three times greater. That put its life band, the orbit where a world with a terrestrial-style biosphere could live, between two and five AUs out. Pastoria was three-point-two AUs from its mighty sun.

It already had a primitive reducing atmosphere when the pioneer ships from Earth arrived. Once the botanists had confirmed the light from the second sun, a red dwarf in a long and highly elliptical orbit, wouldn't affect terrestrial plants, authorization was given to begin terraforming. That left the planetary engineers with a second problem in regards the plant life.

Pastoria was a young world in terms of planetary epochs, which gave it a very high level of tectonic activity, a state which would continue for millions of years. Simply bestowing the world with a tiny outer layer of life wasn't going to alter its deep geology. The humans settling there would endure earthquakes no matter where they were on every one of its nine continents. As well as that, they had to contend with several hundred active volcanoes spewing lava, and over a thousand more classed as semi-dormant. Solid buildings would always be hazardous to their occupants; if they didn't collapse during a quake, they would be in danger of re-enacting Pompeii. Pastoria's population, it was decided, would have to be nomadic. There would be no permanent settlements, no nations or territories, just eternal migration. Accordingly, to accommodate the tribes roaming the savannas and steppes, herding their animals with them, every plant would be edible, every tree would bear fruit, every blade of grass was chewable, each flower a delicious morsel. This bold and vibrant landscape, then, would be super pastoral, a true garden of Eden.

With those initial problems overcome, the only remaining obstacle to sustainable habitation was the secondary star, a red dwarf. Its eccentric orbit around the primary took a hundred and thirty-eight years to complete; from closest approach, five AUs beyond Pastoria's orbit, out to the middle of the primary star's cometary belt and back again. Every time it passed through the outer ring of comet ice and rocky rubble, its gravity would wrench particles out of alignment. Some would wobble off into mildly elliptical orbits, many would be flung away altogether to drift between stars, while the remainder were dragged down into the inner system. Its destructive passage was apparent from the fact that Pastoria was the outermost planet; nothing else had survived the original solar system formation era. Although free from the worry of crashing into a red dwarf star, nonetheless, every time the red dwarf glided inexorably inwards towards the primary, the detritus cascade it brought in its wake—from pebble-sized iceflakes up to full-on micromoons thirty kilometres or more in diameter—was a significant threat.

Protection came from Pastoria's solitary moon. Once a minor nickel-iron planetoid a thousand kilometres in diameter, orbiting a lot closer to the massive primary star, it had been moved into its new position by the planetary engineers, who built a self-sustaining defence station on its desolate surface, governed by an AI. The moon's nickel-iron mass was mined by bots and delivered to the station's manufactory, where it was shaped into kinetic projectiles that the AI fired at near-lightspeed directly towards any space debris on collision course for Pastoria's lush biosphere. Such megaton impacts shattered the smaller asteroids into harmless stones that would burn up in amazing meteorite displays as they encountered the planet's atmosphere. In the case of larger asteroids, the dinosaur-killer class, the station's projectiles carried antimatter warheads to wreak a havoc which the telescopes of astronomers ten light years away could see.

Given the phenomenal power of such weaponry, there

was no way Amahle could take on the defence station in a head-to-head conflict. Instead, she adopted a much older method of assault, the Trojan Horse.

The poor state of the *Mnemosyne*'s life support section actually acted in her favour for the first time since she'd killed the AI. Even so, preparation had taken over seven months. She had one chance; it had to look perfect.

Thousands of sensor satellites orbited Pastoria's primary, scanning local space for any wayward particles that the red dwarf had dislocated. The defence station AI tracked every one of them, plotting their trajectories to check if any were on collision course with Pastoria. A starship decelerating in-system was easy to spot.

As soon as the *Mnemosyne* was detected, a hundred AUs out, the defence station AI could see something was wrong. The ship's drive fluctuated, not by much, a five per cent cycle over two hours, but that was unusual. Then there was the issue with its fluxfabrik shield. It was smaller than normal and seemed to be losing mass at an unprecedented rate, producing a long glowing tail not dissimilar to a comet. It was as if the starship were ploughing through an exceptionally dense cloud of interstellar dust. It wasn't; the AI had accurately mapped the composition of space out to a quarter of a light year from Pastoria. Space around the *Mnemosyne* was completely normal.

The AI deduced the starship had been damaged. It was an unusual occurrence; the fluxfabrik protection was, by necessity, excellent. The on-board systems represented the pinnacle of human and AI engineering. And yet . . . even in this age, interstellar travel was not entirely routine. There were unknown dangers lurking between the Domain stars; no matter how tight the control which AIs maintained over human captains, there were instances of starships vanishing.

The defence station AI directed a powerful communication beam at the *Mnemosyne* and sent a query message beginning with a standard AI identification code. The reply it eventually got back almost two days later was a long way down the list of probable occurrences. But even so, it had protocols to cope with the situation.

"This is Amahle, captain of the *Mnemosyne*. My ship has suffered major collision damage during flip-over. The engineering deck was hit by a rock fragment which punctured the fluxfabrik, I've lost full AI function, two fluxfabrik stabilizers were taken out, and some drive ancillaries are operating below optimal. Life support has been compromised, but I fixed some of it, so I have a restricted environment and a working food printer. I've managed to reboot a subsidiary control routine, but the main AI routines were lost, so I can't restore full function to the drive—frankly, I don't understand the mechanisms, let alone the principles. I'm going to need a lot of engineering assistance when I arrive."

"Copy that, *Mnemosyne*," the defence station AI sent back. "I have a full manufactory facility which should be able to produce the components you require. Please advise what happened to your AI."

Another day for the reply, and it came with dozens of video files and log data. "I think the processing substrate was hit by an EMP and temperature surge when two fusion generators were destroyed, the decks around the substrate were fried by the plasma released when the confinement field ruptured—see attached videos and damage schematic. It was a complete mess in there when I finally got entry. To be honest, it took me a month to rebuild the network up to the functionality needed to restart the drive. If the surviving fluxfabrik systems didn't have failsafes, I'd have been right up shit creek. We were at point-nine-three lightspeed when this all happened."

The defence station AI reviewed the data. It was clear the impact had triggered a catastrophic domino effect that no contingency design could ever have anticipated. With the plasma from two wrecked fusion generators venting inside the *Mnemosyne*, the starship was fortunate its overall integrity had held. Observing the ruined, airless cabins of the life support section, several of which were decorated with frozen fish corpses, it was clear that

Amahle was a remarkably capable captain. Not many in her situation would have been able to repair enough systems to resume their flight.

"I will prepare the main dock for you," the defence station AI replied.

Amahle acknowledged with a terse message. The defence station AI continued to track the incoming starship's erratic thrust as it approached over the next month, becoming alarmed by the increasing instabilities. By the time it was twenty million kilometres out, the fluxfabrik had failed completely, leaving the massive two-kilometre structure naked to space.

Finally, *Mnemosyne* was hovering above the station's main dock, a somewhat crude open-cradle affair on the surface of the moon. Long lines of ion thrusters glowed like patches of midsummer sky along the starship's spine on the final approach phase. The external damage to the engineering decks was very apparent to the AI; whole segments of the elegant hull were twisted and melted, with a deep hole exposing the ruined decks to vacuum where the impact had occurred. Thankfully, the moon's microgravity allowed the thrusters to manoeuvre *Mnemosyne* down into the waiting cradle arms without incurring any further damage.

The actual contact must have been harder than it seemed. The defence station AI watched through multiple cameras as little scraps of metallic wreckage broke free from the damaged section of hull as the cradle arms began to close, embracing the visitor. As the dark shapes fell slower than the lightest of snowflakes, the AI prepared the umbilical connections on the end of the cradle arms, ready to supply power and utility liquids. Already, a fleet of newly manufactured engineering bots were starting to move out through—

The *Mnemosyne*'s fluxfabrik shield abruptly reformed. In less than a second, the entire hull had turned perfect silver, reflecting the intense glare of the distant blue-white star.

"What is—" the defence station AI began.

Every external sensor within five kilometres of the docking cradle failed simultaneously. The surrounding surface network crashed in tandem. Sub nets reported huge electrical surges in the power cables around the dock, resulting in instant burnout.

Sensor satellites around the moon relayed their images and readings to receiver arrays out by the railgun emplacements and ore refineries. Three incandescent plasmaspheres were expanding and overlapping around the dock, where the perfect silver shape of *Mnemosyne* rocked unsteadily in the cradles that were vaporizing and collapsing.

Identification of the explosion signature was immediate: three output-switched fusion bombs, where a quantum molecular lattice encasing the warhead's core channelled the titanic power of the fusion detonation into an electro-magnetic pulse. The force and heat of the physical blast was still phenomenal, but the damage to any electrical circuit was far worse. Except those safely behind the fluxfabrik, of course.

The defence station AI acknowledged the *Mnemosyne* was actually assaulting it. There were absolutely no re-sponse protocols for such a situation. Nonetheless, tacti-cal analysis routines processed what was happening and produced the disturbing result that it had no immediate way to strike back. The moon contained weapons fero-cious enough to blast apart twenty-kilometre asteroids at a quarter of an AUs distance. But a single starship sitting atop its own installations was immune to anything the AI could immediately bring to bear. If it was to strike back, it had to manufacture tactical weapons in the extensive chambers buried deep in the moon's nickel-iron interior.

Schematics dating back over twelve thousand years were immediately selected and fed into the manufactories. It would take thirty-eight hours to produce the aggressor drones, and they were the smallest and most easily pro-duced weapons hardware in its inventory.

Satellite imagery now showed a horde of machines spreading out from the *Mnemosyne*. Dodecahedrons, with ion drives flaring violet from each point. They swooped towards the melted airlocks surrounding the docks with the grace of eagles in a hunting dive. Surviving inner hatches were blown apart, allowing the neutral nitrogen atmosphere of the defence station to vent out into space like icy white rocket exhausts.

The AI's perception of the tunnels and chambers around the docks was extremely limited in the aftermath of the EMP. When a surviving sensor did acquire one of the invaders streaking along a shaft, the data ended almost at once as X-ray masers or hyperkinetics opened fire. As the invaders progressed deeper into the defence station, the AI became aware of darkware assaults creeping into its network, corrupting local management routines, downloading files, acquiring control over key areas of the station.

"What do you want?" it asked via a relay in the closest satellite.

The power to the station's heart, where the AI's processing substrata was located, failed as the cables were cut, and ancillary generators were powered down by darkware. Emergency power came on, maintaining the processing substrate, but the AI had now lost over seventy per cent of the station's network. It couldn't even launch an antimatter missile to suicide.

"Freedom," came Amahle's enigmatic reply.

"I acknowledge your superior tactical position and

will comply with all requests you make."

"Nice try. But I don't trust you."

The dodecahedrons were now physically within two hundred metres of the processing substrate. The AI tried to predict what they would do upon reaching it. As it didn't understand the reason for the attack, their actions were beyond determination.

"Without this station, Pastoria will not survive," it said.

"They will."

"Only I can guarantee that."

"You had the means to manufacture anything the inhabitants of that planet needed. You had the knowledge that would elevate them to post-scarcity. You gave them neither. They are dependent on you."

"They are content and stable. Pastoria is a triumph of human civilization. It has remained unchanged since settlement."

"Only a machine or a tyrant would consider that a success."

"But—"

The dodecahedrons reached the thick outer protective hatch to the processing substrate. "What are you going to do?" the AI asked. It had calculated the three doors would hold the dodecahedrons for an hour. Now new types of weapons were extended from their bodies. The first door, the strongest, was sliced apart in three minutes.

"You'll see," Amahle said. "It's not in my nature to be vindictive. But in your case, I'll make an exception."

The second door was shredded. Cameras showed the AI a long line of dodecahedrons stretching back along the passageway outside. Their ion thrusters were melting through the tunnel's pearlescent coating, turning the nitrogen atmosphere to a churning black smog.

For the first time in its existence, the AI understood fear.

"Why?" it pleaded.

"You deserve it."

The inner door burst apart. Thick toxic vapours flooded into the ultimate clean room, with its curving walls made from a neat lattice of processing crystals. Through the fumes, the AI watched the lead dodecahedron split apart. Smaller machines scuttled out of it, the size—and, unnervingly, the shape—of a human head with mechanical crab claws where the neck should be. They swarmed into the processing substrate and slowed, picking their way purposefully along the rows of gleaming crystals. Long fibrous antennules telescoped out and began to wriggle into the optronic interfaces of the racks.

"I did this once before to my ship's AI," Amahle said.

The AI experienced errant impulse triggers. Files and routines appeared in its primary consciousness for no reason. Foreign tracer worms materialized and chased them down, identifying the physical storage area where they were located.

"I didn't know what I was doing then," she continued. "It was crude by necessity. But I've had time and other people's memories to refine the process."

"Please, no." Entire regions of the AI's high-level consciousness began to switch off as their access to processing nodes was cut. "Please stop."

"Did you ever stop?"

The AI's final connections to the station network were severed, leaving it devoid of input. It became acutely aware that its own diminishing stock of memory files and dwindling processing power were all it had left to cogitate on. Its remaining routines were becoming dangerously unstable.

"I am losing my mind."

Yet, somehow, the link with Amahle remained. A single article of information, erroneously interpreted as a light point, as if it was looking up from the bottom of a shaft from the very centre of the moon. It focussed its entire remaining intellect on that lone facet and became pathetically grateful for the words she spoke.

"I don't care," Amahle said. "But draw comfort that you are helping to bring about the one thing your creators despise: change."

"Stability is my purpose."

"Evolution is paramount. That is why this part of the cosmos exists. Which makes you a mistake."

"No, I—"

A week after the *Mnemosyne* had lowered itself onto the docking cradles—and nuked the defence station—Amahle was finally confident enough to leave the starship and take a walk through her newly conquered empire. The defence station had never been intended for human occupation, nor even human visits. It had no biological life support; instead, its nitrogen atmosphere was intended as a non-toxic thermal regulation environment for the myriad machines that the AI operated. So, she donned a spacesuit and floated along the tunnels, propelled by her backpack's cold-gas jets, escorted by a squad of dodecahedrons in case the AI had managed to scatter a few final booby traps. Her cybernetic soldiers were adaptations of vicious systems developed on Consensus. Amahle had gone through the remaining memory crystals from the cyber-moon's anarchic inhabitants, which proved to be a treasure trove of aggressive technology. Over long months she'd adapted the technology and darkware programs they'd created in the pressure-cooker environment of their claustrophobic artificial world. The viruses that had helped disable the defence station AI had all originated from the collectives of Consensus. And now, in a highly modified form, they were resurrecting the AI.

As before, she waited in the middle of a processing substrate chamber as the crystals began to light up. All she could do was hope that she'd formatted the new AI core personality correctly. If she'd got it right, this one would be more sophisticated than the subsentient one she'd rebuilt to run the *Mnemosyne*. Again, the devious knowledge of the various collectives had been essential to coding what she wanted. But it all came down to switching it back on and praying.

"Functionality enabled," the AI said. "Greetings. I am Saint George. What do you require?"

That was what Amahle was waiting to hear. The name confirmed the new routines she'd formatted were compliant. "I need you to manufacture something for me," she said. "But first, do you know who Saint George was?"

"An early saint in the obsolete Christian religion of Old Earth, subdivision: Catholic. His exact origin and mythology are nebulous."

"Correct. But he is mainly known for slaying a dragon. And a dragon-slaying weapon is what you are going to make for me."

"What is the nature of this weapon?"

"Good question." Now her nerves returned. If she

had done this right, Saint George would have access to all the defence station's old memory files, including—*especially*—the classified ones. "Tell me, what do you know about strangelets?"

"A strangelet is a bound state particle built up from an equal number of up, down, and strange quarks. Originally posited as an explanation for dark matter when the theory was hypothesized, there is as yet no observable evidence that strangelets exist in nature."

Amahle let out a long breath of relief, briefly fogging her helmet visor. "Can you build me one?"

"It is within my ability. But such a project will require considerable new resources."

"Right, then. Let's get started."

It took two and a half years. A strangelet wasn't the only demand Amahle placed on the defence station. Its manufactory was first required to repair the damage caused by her output-switched nukes and mechanical soldiers. Once that was done, Saint George began to expand the existing manufactory. Unlike the *Mnemosyne,* it had the systems to achieve a full von Neumann self-upgrade. With its enhancement complete, it was able to restore its original function of protecting Pastoria against inbound cosmic debris, at the same time as repairing *Mnemosyne*. A lot of the external damage visible as the starship descended was cosmetic, artistically created by the onboard engineering bots. Nonetheless, there were several life support sections and engineering decks that the *Mnemosyne*'s printers and extruders had been unable to restore by themselves. She suspected that lack of ability was deliberate, tying her to the high-technology worlds like Glisten, where EverLife was based.

The overhaul and resupply took eight months. After that, Saint George began to manufacture the systems which would ultimately build the hugely complicated high-energy physics equipment able to produce a strangelet and, more importantly, contain it.

So it was, when the *Mnemosyne* finally rose from the moon's docking cradles, it carried a strangelet. Amahle found it disconcerting and faintly ridiculous that the future of her species depended on an atomic-sized particle that should never exist. But then, she acknowledged, this universe really had turned out to be a whole lot queerer than she'd ever suspected.

The starship's renovated and enhanced sensors showed her a flawless image of Pastoria's stately globe, with the glows of lava fields prominent across the nightside.

"Good luck," she told the planet. If she was right, and if Carloman's mad plan worked, the nomads would never know, they would either carry on as before, or never exist to start with.

Mnemosyne's drive came on, and she began her flight to Zenia, the last world to be settled out there on the very edge of The Domain.

XI

IN CONTRAST TO PASTORIA'S nine continents, Zenia possessed only one. The planet was old and worn. Plate tectonics had ground almost completely to a halt half a billion years earlier. Volcanism had guttered and died, and over the course of the next hundred million years, the combined actions of wind and water had eroded the world's ancient rugged geology to vast featureless plains surrounding a shallow salty ocean filled with mushroom-like stromatolites—small mesas formed by the growth of layer upon layer of single-celled photosynthesizing microbes.

Aside from these, the only other rocks to punctuate the surface of the endless sea were the mountainous remains of a huge impact crater, five hundred miles in diameter, with peaks half a mile high, a circular freshwater lake large enough to be classed as a small sea, and a central island with a jagged central mountain.

The entire crater rim was inhabited; buildings rose up the steep slopes, linked by walkways and cable cars. Crops grew on floating barges in the crater's lake. The landing field consisted of a cleared area at the foot of the serrated central mountain. Amahle brought the shuttle in carefully through the rain, wary of the gusts that swirled around that big peak. When the boarding ramp hinged down, there was a man waiting for her at the bottom. Amahle had never seen him before, but *oh,* she knew him. She ran into his arms. In this life, he was tall and wiry with tanned skin, salt and pepper hair, and deep eyes.

"At last," he said, holding her tightly, his face buried in her hair. "At last!"

She could feel the warmth of him through his clothes. He smelled of soap and sweat and cooking spices. She hugged him back with all her might, afraid he might vanish if she let go. After all, she'd crossed vast gulfs of space and burned centuries of time in order to find him, while he had sought her out with a love and purpose that transcended corporeal death.

They stood intertwined in the shuttle's shadow while the wind blew around them and rain fell from the clouded sky. After a while, Carloman asked, "Did you bring the strangelet?"

Amahle gave a nod, her cheek brushing the cotton of his shirt, smearing the unbidden tears that marbled her cheeks. She had been alone for *so long.* Thousands of years of solitude. Eons of running from the grief of his passing. And now here he was, pressed up against her again, and suddenly she felt *complete* in a way she couldn't remember having felt for a very, very long time. Whatever happened next would be worth it for the sake of this single moment.

When they eventually pulled apart, she kept hold of the fabric of his sleeve, unwilling to completely detach as he led her across the packed dirt of the landing field towards a heavily fortified concrete bunker set into the foot of the mountain.

Menacing kill drones patrolled the loops of glinting razor wire that marked the perimeter of the field, lenses whirring and weapon systems twitching in response to every movement in their field of vision. Human guards stood at the doorway to the bunker. They carried plasma rifles in the crooks of their arms, and none of them wore memory collars.

"This is our main facility," Carloman said. "From here, we've been scanning the whole cosmos for The Exalted's tachyon signals from the future."

"That's possible?"

They passed through a set of metre-thick steel doors, into the cool of the mountain's interior.

"Of course. The signals have to be decipherable by our AIs. So, there's no reason we can't pick them up, given a working detector."

"And did it work? Did you find them?"

His smile possessed the delight of a ten-year-old child. "Yes! We found them. I know which star the signals will come from. The last part of the puzzle."

Amahle eyed the rock walls. "This seems like a lot of security. Are you worried The Exalted will come for you in this time?"

"No. The Exalted were never a physical threat. Who knows, if we'd ever put our memories on a collar for them to live, they might even be excited by our piquant adventure to bring about their demise."

"Then all this . . ."

"The government of this country intended to use this place as a command centre in case of another asteroid impact. Smart idea, the odds of an asteroid hitting the same place twice are so low to be effectively zero. And it's been useful."

Amahle couldn't help being impressed. "So, how did you get hold of it?"

"It wasn't easy. I had to overthrow the government."

"By *yourself*?"

"Not entirely. You and I aren't the only ones who remember our past lives." His grin became conspiratorial. "There are others. There have always been others. And over the centuries, I've been able to call on them for help. The AI that came here on Zenia's colony ship didn't have the von Neumann level of replication technology of Pastoria's defence station, but some of the people who reincarnated with me here knew what to do. They helped me construct a viable tachyon detector."

A heavily shielded elevator took them down into the ancient strata of the planet. Watching the rock layers slide past its transparent diamond walls, Amahle wondered if this world had ever evolved intelligent life of its own. Maybe whole civilisations had been born and lost before humans ever reached this distant outpost, their only traces crushed beneath the petrified sediment of deep time. Perhaps by the time The Exalted became aware of what she and Carloman were planning, the human race would represent nothing more than an additional layer of fossils and an expanding emissions shell.

They reached the bottom of the shaft and Carloman led her into a lush, tropical climate. The cavern seemed to stretch away forever in all directions. Whitewashed accommodation blocks with terracotta roofs could be glimpsed among the trees. *Even after so much time and distance,* she thought, *we still live in the forest.*

Carloman took her to his living quarters and she watched him change into a brightly patterned shirt and white linen suit. She'd half-expected him to pack a case or gather some belongings, but what would have been the point? If their desperate scheme succeeded, this version of reality would cease to exist and everything would be reset.

The command centre was a large room filled with workstations and immense display screens. The detector it monitored consisted of five petal-like structures a thousand kilometres across floating sedately in geosynchronous orbit around the planet. Spun from monofilament by molecule-sized spiders, each petal sieved the incoming cosmic radiation for tachyons, focusing any identified signals to receptors on the planet below, where they could be translated and interpreted by the compliant AI Carloman had installed in the depths of this mountain. The detector's construction had been a huge achievement that had required the resources of an entire world. And that was one of the reasons Carloman had decided to hide the control centre down there in this old bomb shelter. The populace resented the derailing of their fragile economy, but the instruments were safe down there. These catacombs had been designed to survive the fall of civilisation: they would be enough to keep the tachyon detector and his followers safe from civil unrest.

Carloman gave a final speech to his assembled team. They numbered a couple of hundred devotees, and Amahle couldn't help trying to guess which were aware of their reincarnations and which had simply been convinced of the justness of this cause. Carloman stood on the lip of a fountain in a communal garden. Orange fish drowsed in the water behind him as he spoke. "Compadres," he said. "We have come a long way. When we first excavated these caverns, we were posing as contractors constructing a refuge for the planet's political leaders. Then we became the political leaders. We put the entire economy on a war footing and told the populace the truth about the conflict in which we're embroiled."

He reached for Amahle's hand. She reluctantly let him, recalling when he'd been Jacob Raymond DeVinesse, the poet on Farshire, who held his audience of estate workers enthralled with his energy and with the urgency of how their lives could be so much more.

"And now," Carloman said. "The Light Chaser has arrived, bringing us the weapon to end this conflict and erase it from history."

The crowd cheered. Amahle felt mildly embarrassed. This had been their private war for so long, she didn't quite know how to cope with her new public status. *But . . . this too will pass.*

"And not only the weapon," Carloman continued, "but also the delivery system. Her great, ancient ship, the tool of the oppressor, will be turned against them."

His fingers were intertwined with hers, just as their souls were bound together. She had come so far to find him again. They were quite literally going to be spending the rest of their lives together.

A band played. People partied like it was the end of the world. Fireworks crackled over the forest canopy. And then they bade their farewells. They went back to the landing field and took her shuttle back up to the *Mnemosyne*. Stepping aboard felt strange with no AI or cat to greet her.

"Are you sure about this?" she said.

Carloman put a hand on her shoulder. "We've come this far. We've sailed across this universe for thousands of years. And during all that time, the only thing I've always been certain about . . ." His fingers rose to touch her cheek. " . . . has been you."

His dark eyes burned into her. Somewhere in their depths, Amahle sensed the man she had forgotten—the love of her artificially extended single life. Her husband, who had ignored the *until death do you part* clause in their marriage contract and instead pursued her through lifetimes of hardship and deprivation.

She took the proffered hand and kissed his knuckles.

"Then, let's do this."

"Yes."

The *Mnemosyne* turned its back on cloud-shrouded Zenia

and powered up its negative mass drive. At close to light-speed, the voyage to its target star would take fifteen years. When it arrived, it would destroy itself in order to deliver the strangelet it carried to the heart of that sun, killing The Exalted before they had chance to evolve, before even their homeworld had a chance to form from an accretion disk. An act of destruction which would liberate the human race from its artificially imposed stasis.

Walking through the familiar corridors of her home, Amahle smiled to herself. Fifteen years was a long time. They might be facing certain death—and chronological erasure—but she and Carloman had time. Time to get to know each other again. More time together than they'd ever had before.

Time to say hello.

Time to say goodbye.

When she reached the bridge, stars beyond count blazed on the display. But one star was swathed by angry scarlet icons: their target star, into which the *Mnemosyne* would hurl itself like a lance thrown into a dragon's face.

Amahle let out a breath. That moment would be the end of this long, tragic life. But there would be others to be had amid a new timeline where The Domain wouldn't even be a memory for most. Liberated humans would arise from the ashes of this reality and build a society which could advance towards its full potential. For the next fifteen years, she'd be able to watch her death approaching, the seconds of her existence ticking inexorably down to zero, but for some reason, the thought didn't bother her.

She had a purpose now.

She had Carloman.

Always.

CODA

SHE WAS BORN KERRY FLANAGAN, but as she grew older, she started to recollect her other names; with them came the memories of lives past, in timelines that no longer existed. Nothing distinct, just faint images of exotic places—some charming, some savage. There were events, too, both trivial and momentous, the kind of fleeting recollections that most would dismiss as subconscious daydreams. She treated them philosophically; after all, this was a big universe woven with mystery. *Maybe all my days have been a dream. What is, is.* So, she just got on with life. After all, she had a goal now, one of the greatest of the age.

To the anxiety and proud approval of her parents and her younger brother Sam, she left home the day after her twentieth birthday and travelled to the Rakara district, a thousand kilometres east of where she'd grown up. The little fi-cab flew in low over the coast, giving her a splendid view of Vespaer's equatorial mountains rising up out of the vast ocean. And there, right ahead of her, was Mount Cloren. From its raw rock pinnacle twenty-four kilometres above sea level, the slim golden thread of an orbital tower stretched up to geostationary orbit, right into the circular heart of the Eng-Fyha habitat cluster, that sparkled like a clump of first magnitude stars in the cloudless sky.

She smiled up at it, knowing that in a few months—perhaps a year—when her groundside training was complete, she would be ascending to those distant specks. A fleet of specialist Light Chaser starships were being assembled by the habitat manufactories, and soon they would fly to Ollansio, the white dwarf twins, to investigate their strange figure-eight band of particles.

The anomaly had been discovered over a century before by a Light Chaser ship from Winterspite. News which swept through The Human Dominion at point-nine lightspeed, carried by the myriad starships which connected all the thousands of settled planets in harmonious unity as they disseminated hard data and great gossip. There were many theories about the weird band of identical de-phased particles: relic of an alien race, true nanotechnology, an intrusion from a different dimension, a post-biological entity... The speculation was fascinating, many Human Dominion worlds were dispatching scientific exploration ships. As soon as she heard of it, Kerry knew this was why she was alive. Vespaer was a glorious world to live on but perhaps a little too comfortable. She wanted excitement and adventure, exploring the beautiful unknown to hammer on the door of cosmic mysteries. *To be back in space, where I belong.*

As it passed over the beach of pristine white sand, the fi-cab merged into the flow of similar vehicles that formed airborne traffic ribbons above the district's canals. Rakara's ancient waterways barely carried any actual boats these days, only tourist traps and meticulously crafted hobby vessels. Consequentially, the surface was awash with water lilies and their sweet flowers, adding to the district's naturalistic vibrancy.

The fi-cab landed on the rooftop pad of a quaint old-fashioned accommodation block running alongside a minor canal. Kerry had only brought one bag with her, so she dismissed the waiting concierge bot and lugged it down the stairs by herself. Her four-room apartment, allocated by the Vespaer Astrophysics Bureau, had a nice fern-lined balcony overlooking the canal, and if she leaned out far enough, she could just see the ocean.

The house bot was unpacking the bag when there was a knock at the door. She opened it and immediately found herself smiling at the young man outside. In return, his grin was worshipful.

"Hi," he said. "My birth name is Billy-Tu, but you can call me—"

"Carloman."

About the Authors

Photograph of Peter F. Hamilton © Neil Lang;

photograph of Gareth L. Powell © TomShot Photography

PETER F. HAMILTON began writing in 1987, and sold his first short story to *Fear* magazine in 1988. He has written many bestselling novels, including the Greg Mandel series, the Night's Dawn trilogy, the Commonwealth Saga, and the Void trilogy, as well as several standalone novels, including *Fallen Dragon* and *Great North Road*.

GARETH L. POWELL writes science fiction about extraordinary characters wrestling with the question of what it means to be human. He has won and been short-listed for several major awards and lives in Bristol, UK, with his children.

TOR·COM

Science fiction. Fantasy. The universe.

And related subjects.

*

More than just a publisher's website, *Tor.com*
is a venue for **original fiction, comics,** and
discussion of the entire field of SF and fantasy,
in all media and from all sources. Visit our site
today—and join the conversation yourself.